A FOOLISH WAGER

THE SPINSTERS GUILD (BOOK 4)

ROSE PEARSON

A FOOLISH WAGER

The Spinsters Guild

(Book 4)

By

Rose Pearson

A FOOLISH WAGER

"*L*ady Amelia, come down from there at once!"

Lady Amelia did nothing but giggle and climb higher, choosing quite firmly to ignore the anxious voice of her governess. She had climbed this particular tree on many previous occasions and certainly was not about to stop doing so now!

"You must desist!" her governess called, now sounding both angry and upset. "Your father will be greatly displeased."

Amelia grimaced and placed her hand on a higher branch. She knew very well that her father, the Earl of Stockbridge, was not at home at present and certainly would not care about what she had been doing given he showed her very little interest. She reminded him too much of her mother, who had died giving birth to Amelia some twelve years ago.

"Please!" her governess called as Amelia climbed higher, with an even greater determination than before. "Do stop, Lady Amelia. You must come down."

Amelia said nothing, holding onto a firm branch and swinging one leg up and over a thick branch she fully intended to sit on. From this height, she would be able to see across the whole estate and, if she continued to ignore her governess, might find a few minutes of enjoyment.

Unfortunately, Amelia's skirts and petticoats—which she had done her best to sweep out of the way of her feet —decided not to do as Amelia wished. They chose, instead, to become entangled, meaning she could not easily lift her foot up and over the branch.

Her breath caught, her hands tightening on the branch whilst her other foot teetered on the thinner branch below. Her foot was well and truly caught, and she could not let go of her grasp on the tree to sort herself out.

"Lady Amelia!"

Her governess sounded afraid now, perhaps able to see the difficulty Amelia was in. "Will you please come down!"

Amelia tried to shout for help, feeling her hands slip as she tried her best to remove her foot from her skirts. And then, before she knew it, she was falling.

Falling was meant to be painless, but Amelia felt as though she bounced off every single tree branch as she fell. The breath was thrown from her body as she landed, hard, hearing a sickening crack that seemed to come not from the tree, but from her.

And then, her governess started to scream. Amelia wanted to tell her to be quiet, wanted to say she was quite all right and had only fallen a little way, but found she could not seem to say a single word. It was as though she were caught between wakefulness and a dream, not able to speak and certainly not able to move.

Pain began to spread through Amelia's body as she lay on the grass, her governess still screaming for help. Blinking rapidly against the agony, Amelia sucked in air, trying to push the pain away, trying to force it down, but it only continued to grow and grow within her, until a scream left her lips and began to join in with the cries of her governess. Her leg began to burn with a deep and furious pain and, as she lifted her head just a little to look at it, Amelia realized, with horror, it now sat at a very strange angle indeed.

Throwing her head back against the grass, Amelia screamed again, in both pain and fear. Her governess was speaking rapidly to someone—the gardener, perhaps—but this did not bring Amelia any comfort from her agony.

"We shall have the surgeon here very soon, Lady Amelia," she heard her governess say as a whimper began to leave her throat, replacing the screams. "You shall be quite all right, I am sure of it."

Amelia began to cry, hot tears slipping down her cheeks as she opened her eyes to see her governess, ashen-faced, kneeling beside her.

"Do not fear," her governess continued, her smile tremulous as she pressed one hand lightly on Amelia's forehead. "You will be well again very soon, Lady Amelia. There may be pain for a while, but soon, it will go, and you will be yourself again. You will just have to be brave for a time. Do you think you can do that?"

Amelia closed her eyes again and began to sob. The pain seemed to be a part of her now as though it would never fully allow her to escape from it and, despite the comforting words of her governess, Amelia began to think she would never fully escape this agony, feeling it take a firm hold of her frame.

"They are coming now," the governess continued, wiping Amelia's tears. "You shall have to be very brave now, Lady Amelia, but we shall soon have you inside and in bed, where you will begin to recover. Have no fear. It will all be over very soon."

CHAPTER ONE

"This is to be the year you are wed, Amelia."

Lady Amelia shook her head but lowered her gaze, knowing she could not contradict her uncle. Her father, the previous Earl of Stockbridge, had passed away some three years ago, and as such, his brother and her uncle, had taken the title. After her year of mourning, her uncle had accompanied her to London for her first season, which had not gone well at all. This now being her second season, he clearly expected her to find a husband just as soon as she could.

"I am certain there is someone within society who will take another look at you, especially when it is known that you have an ever greater dowry than last season," he continued authoritatively. "And besides, it is not as though you are...unbecoming."

Amelia resisted the urge to roll her eyes, knowing very well that she might be a diamond of the first water, but her limp marred her considerably. Yes, she knew very well that she had a fine figure and her very dark hair and emerald eyes were striking, but none of that caught a gentleman's attention. The moment she took a step out onto the floor, they would look to her limp and all interest would evaporate.

"Mrs. Peters will continue to be your companion, of course," the Earl continued, referring to Amelia's companion who had been a stalwart during last year's season. "And she will do all she can to direct you towards a suitable gentleman."

"Yes, Uncle," Amelia replied without hesitation, knowing this was the response she was expected to give.

"And whilst you may struggle to dance, you must force yourself to do everything you can," her uncle directed, his thick, graying eyebrows lowering down as his dark green eyes sharpened themselves upon her. "You must not remain in the shadows, Amelia."

"No, Uncle." Amelia had never wanted to be the center of attention and had done all she could last season to make herself invisible, but evidently, her uncle had been aware of this. It had not done much good, of course, for everyone knew there was a young lady who had a bad limp amongst them. It did not matter whether or not she had a good title or an excellent dowry. The flaw was all the *beau monde* saw.

"Very good." The Earl cleared his throat, drawing himself up to his full height and reminding Amelia once again of the intimidating figure her uncle could be. He had never shown her any particular care or consideration, just as her father had done, and had taken on a similar attitude to her limp. Her father had always blamed her for her limp without once understanding it had been nothing more than an accident, and her uncle considered this to be the case also. It was as if Amelia had done so on purpose, as though she had deliberately brought this calamity upon herself to make life more than a little difficult for her family. There had been no acknowledgment that it had just been a childish caper, no seeming acceptance that to climb a tree was something all children sought to do—especially if it meant they were able to escape their lessons in doing so! She could still remember how her father had loomed over her bed as she had lain there in agony, her leg being splinted by the less-than-gentle surgeon. He had shown her no sympathy, had given her no words of compassion. Instead, there had been a harsh rebuke and outright anger over what she had done. Amelia had felt such guilt and shame that she had turned away from her father entirely and had done so ever since then. There had never been any joy in being in his presence, never any happiness. Instead, there just came the same dull feeling of guilt, the same unhappiness, and the same sense of grief that there had never been familial care for each other between herself and the Earl. It was made all the more pertinent now by the fact that he was gone from this world and had left her entirely at the mercy of her uncle—who wanted her gone from under his roof just as soon as possible.

"I will inform Mrs. Peters as to your upcoming events and the invitations you have received," the Earl finished, turning and walking towards the door. "You are to attend Lord Marston's ball this evening, so ensure you are quite prepared."

Amelia bobbed a quick curtsy but said nothing,

feeling a lump in her throat that could not be easily removed. When the door closed behind her uncle, she let out a long breath, hearing the sob within it but choosing to ignore it completely. There was no good in crying now, not when it would come to naught. There were expectations she had to fulfill, regardless of the pain within her heart. Her uncle did not care for her feelings, and neither, it seemed, must she. She was expected to do as he wished without hesitation and now, it seemed, was to seek out any gentleman of both good breeding and decent fortune in order to make herself amenable to them. It did not matter what she thought of each of the gentlemen, did not matter whether or not they were kind, compassionate, foul-tempered, or arrogant. She would have to take whatever she could. Should a gentleman show even the slightest flicker of interest, then Amelia knew she would be expected to encourage his attention, whether or not she found the gentleman interesting or agreeable.

"It seems we have our orders," Mrs. Peters murmured, rising from a chair in the corner of the room and reminding Amelia that she had been present for the Earl's conversation. She had entirely forgotten her companion was in the room at all, for Mrs. Peters—whilst determined, with a strong character and a firmness about her gaze, was fairly diminutive. Turning, Amelia put on a smile she did not feel and tried to shrug.

"Indeed," she said as nonchalantly as she could. "My uncle has expectations, and I must do my best to fulfill them."

Mrs. Peters drew near and put a hand on Amelia's shoulder, comforting her. "I know you find his demands very difficult indeed," she said kindly, making Amelia's eyes burn with unshed tears. "But you do very well to tolerate him. You know I am here to do my very best to help you."

Amelia nodded, the smile fading from her face as a lump began to settle in her throat. She could not speak for fear that she would begin to cry, aware Mrs. Peters knew of her failure from last season. Mrs. Peters had been a good deal more callous towards Amelia at the beginning of last season, having been chosen by the Earl to ensure Amelia found a husband. It had been a practical matter, Mrs. Peters had said, nothing more. But, as the season had gone on and Mrs. Peters had seen how the *ton* had stared at Amelia, how they had whispered about her and how she had slowly been left feeling nothing but embarrassment and shame, something had changed. Mrs. Peters had softened towards Amelia, standing beside her in solidarity and understanding. She had felt Amelia's pain and had encouraged her as best she could to remain unblinking and unaffected by it, even though Amelia had been unable to do so. This season, Amelia was quite certain Mrs. Peters would continue to be as kind and as supportive as she had been at the last.

"I do not know how I am to fulfill my uncle's demands," Amelia whispered, her heart beginning to ache within her. "I am nothing but a figure of fun when it comes to the *ton*. You know very well they do not see me once they see my limp."

Mrs. Peters nodded, not hiding the truth from Amelia. "I am aware this is what they see, but I cannot agree that it is all that you are," she said gently. "You must not allow yourself to believe you are, somehow, less worthy than other young ladies of the *ton*. That is not true. You have a small limp, yes, but that does not detract from your wonderful qualities. It is the *ton*'s failing that does not seek out such things from you, Amelia. Do not permit them to break your spirit."

Amelia closed her eyes, forcing back her tears. "I do not think I know what to do," she said hoarsely, feeling her spirits quail. "Am I just to go about society as I have done before, hoping someone will look at me?"

Mrs. Peters sighed, tilting her head. "No," she said after a moment, as Amelia opened her eyes and moved to sit down heavily in a chair, her leg beginning to pain her. "No, I think we must consider a new way of going about things."

"What, then?" Amelia asked, aware she sounded a little desperate but having no shame about such a feeling. "What can we do that will bring me any sort of success?"

Mrs. Peters hesitated, a frown forming between her brows. Amelia watched her closely, not wanting to miss a single word. Mrs. Peters was precisely the opposite of Amelia when it came to their coloring. Mrs. Peters had fair hair, with very light blue eyes, in severe contrast to Amelia's dark hair and green eyes. Mrs. Peters was shorter than Amelia, with a straight, thin figure that held no curve at all, whilst Amelia was both tall and curvaceous. It was certainly a striking contrast, and one Amelia knew had already been mentioned by the *ton* on some occasions. Not that such a thing mattered, for Mrs. Peters had been married to a distant relative of the Earl and, as such, did not have any requirement to show familial similarities. Mrs. Peters had been employed as a companion for Amelia until the time came for Amelia to marry—and she had taken the post gratefully, given her husband was no longer of this world, and she had two children to care for. The children were being cared for by Mrs. Peters' older sister, from what Amelia understood, but Amelia knew very well that Mrs. Peters missed them dreadfully. That brought her even more guilt, for if she were able to make a match quickly, then Mrs. Peters would be able to return to her children all the sooner—and Amelia had every intention of ensuring Mrs. Peters was sent some money each and every month from Amelia herself, in gratitude for her help.

But all that would come once Amelia had found a suitor, which still seemed like an insurmountable mountain standing right in front of her.

"I think we must introduce you to a few ladies," Mrs. Peters said slowly, interrupting Amelia's thoughts. "That might be best."

"To ladies?" Amelia repeated, quite confused. "Do you mean there will be ladies present who have eligible sons?"

Mrs. Peters shook her head. "No, that is not what I mean. I think we should introduce you to ladies that are well established within the *ton*. If they accept you, if they show their willingness to greet you and to converse with you, then the beau monde might be less inclined to see you only for your limp and nothing more."

Amelia blinked rapidly, trying to understand what Mrs. Peters meant. "You think they would aid me in my struggles?"

"I think they *might* do so," Mrs. Peters said quickly. "You know very well what the *ton* are like, Amelia. The ladies of the *ton* can be equally as fickle, and indeed, there are those we shall have to take great pains to avoid!" Her brow furrowed all the more. "Those who love nothing more than to gossip, to spread rumors and to do nothing other than to whisper maliciously about others." Her jaw set, leaving Amelia with no doubt as to what the lady herself thought of such creatures. "I will not stand for it, of course, so therefore we must remain far away from such ladies. However, I am quite certain there are those within the beau monde who would aid you significantly, should we seek them out. We must be wise, of course, but I do think it would be a good endeavor, Amelia."

Amelia managed to smile, thinking to herself that this was, at least, a better idea than to try to make her way through society, grasping at any gentleman she could. "Thank you, Mrs. Peters," she said gratefully. "That does give me a little more hope."

"I am certain we shall find a gentleman of integrity," Mrs. Peters said with a satisfied air. "They may be hiding in the shadows, such as you yourself are inclined to do, but we shall seek them out. I will do all I can to speak to other companions so I might know of any such gentlemen in their considerations. That may give us a little advantage also."

"We can but hope," Amelia replied a little sadly.

"And you must not think that you are the only lady in the beau monde who has such difficulties," Mrs. Peters finished, going to ring the bell before sitting back down.

"You are not, Amelia." Her hands gently clasped in her lap, Mrs. Peters gave Amelia a small yet determined smile. "There will be other young ladies who find themselves in a similar situation, I am certain. They will keep to the shadows and hide from the *ton* as best they can, seeing it more as an enemy than a friend. You need not think that you are alone. In fact!" Her face brightened. "We should ensure that you have some close acquaintances, Amelia! Those who may feel as you do, for that would be an encouragement to you, would it not? You would have the gift of knowing you are not as alone as you believe yourself to be, whilst being able to talk openly about the trials and struggles you face."

Amelia did not know what to say, fearing such a thing might only bring her more sorrow rather than the encouragement Mrs. Peters believed it would.

"Then we have a plan!" Mrs. Peters finished, not allowing Amelia even a moment to speak. "I feel a good deal better now, going forward. This evening shall be our first foray into society, and we shall ensure we are careful and cautious in everything we do and say. You have nothing to fear, Amelia. Trust me when I say this Season will be a good deal more than the last."

There was such a hope in Mrs. Peters' eyes, such a resolution in her voice and expression, that Amelia could find nothing to say. She did not want to state that she found the ideas expressed to be a little far-fetched, nor that she thought they would come to naught. Instead, she smiled, nodded, and tried to accept that what Mrs. Peters said was true. No hope entered her heart, however. All she could recall was last season, when she had seen the eyes watching her limp across the room and heard the whispers coming from behind opened fans. The *ton* was a cruel creature indeed, and Amelia did not want to return to it.

And yet you must, said a small voice within her, as the door opened to reveal a maid carrying a tea tray, which Amelia knew would have a few of her favorite cakes on it also. The staff was always kind to her, and for that, she was more than grateful.

"We shall eat and then take the carriage into town," Mrs. Peters said decisively as the maid set down the tray. "We must find you a few new gowns—at least, that is what your uncle has demanded—and so we shall do precisely that." She smiled brightly at Amelia, who did not feel any of the same hope nor happiness Mrs. Peters seemed to exude. "And you shall be more than beautiful, Amelia. Of that, I am quite certain."

"I thank you," Amelia murmured, reaching forward to pour the tea so she would not have to continue the conversation. If she were to say anything, it would be to remind Mrs. Peters that it did not matter what she looked like; the *ton* would immediately remember her from the previous season, and it would not be because of how she looked. It would be due to her leg and her limp. That was all. The beau monde had a long memory, it seemed, and would cling to its cruelty for as long as it could.

Her heart sank all the more as Mrs. Peters began to express delight at returning to Lord Marston's ball this evening. She reminded Amelia of their foray into society last season, which had begun with the very same ball. Amelia could feel nothing but dread as she considered returning there, feeling her anxiety begin to swirl through her, chasing away any desire for honey cakes or the like that the cook had sent up. This evening was, Amelia was quite sure, bound to go very badly indeed. Even if she kept her chin lifted and her resolve determined, there would be nothing but mockery waiting for her, even if it was kept as silent as could be. The *ton* would not welcome her. Gentlemen would not consider her. Most likely, she would end up as nothing more than a spinster. Given what had happened to her father, Amelia had come to town a few years later than most debutantes and now time was slipping away from her. Her future was as dark as Amelia had ever seen it, leaving her with no hope whatsoever. Even with Mrs. Peters' plans and her good intentions, it seemed there was nothing but sorrow and mortification ahead of her.

Amelia was quite certain she would end up alone, no matter what was attempted. She would fail entirely, and it was, she knew, all her fault.

CHAPTER TWO

"*A*nd just how many conquests are you going to make this year?"

Oliver raised one eyebrow, grinning at his friend. "I do not think I shall divulge any of my intentions to you," he said as Lord Marston began to chuckle loudly. "For I know very well what you shall do with them."

Lord Marston grinned, still chuckling as he shook his head. "I do not know what you mean."

"You do indeed!" Oliver retorted with a broad grin. "I am quite certain this ball has been paid for entirely with the money you made betting on me last season."

Lord Marston shrugged, his face still alight with smiles. "But that should bring you contentment, should it not?" he asked, nudging Oliver with his elbow. "I am your friend, am I not? Therefore, it is quite right that I should make money from you."

Oliver let out a bark of laughter, thinking his friend was just as ridiculous as ever. "I think there would be a good deal of mutterings if you were to make as much money this season, given you betted solely on my achieving certain things," he replied, his grin growing all the more. "Although I will not say I did not enjoy fulfilling certain...expectations."

"Indeed, I should think you did," Lord Marston replied, looking speculatively at Oliver. "Are you certain you cannot give me even a hint of which ladies you are regarding this season?"

"No," Oliver replied firmly, his smile beginning to fade. "I shall not." The truth was, as much as Oliver had found some humor in last season's betting, he did not want such a thing to continue. There was a twinge of humiliation about it as though everything he did and everything he said was being watched by the gentlemen of the *ton*, who would then go on to place a bet in Whites' betting book about whether or not he would be able to seduce a particular lady into giving him her affections. Not that he took any of the debutantes to bed, for he would not ruin them in that sense—but he would not pretend he had not stolen a kiss or two. The rich young widows were quite another thing, of course, but even that had not been safe from the betting book. No, Oliver was quite determined his name would not even enter the book this season. Either he would have to behave impeccably, which was something he did not wish to do at all, or he would have to ensure he did not achieve any of the bets placed within the book itself. That, he hoped, would stop gentlemen from watching his every move so that they might place a wager. He did not want to continue to be nothing more than entertainment.

"I do hope you are not a little out of sorts this

evening," Lord Marston said mildly, as Oliver's hand gripped his glass a little tighter. "You know very well it is all in jest, Montague."

Oliver let out a slow breath, hoping his friend did not see him do so. Some of his tension began to uncoil, his shoulders slumping just a little. "Of course," he said, a little less frustrated now. "It is just that I feel as though my life is nothing more than entertainment for those who insist upon watching me."

Lord Marston shrugged as though he did not think this was a particularly difficult concern.

"I do not like being sport," Oliver said firmly. "That is all. I do hope you are understanding, Marston."

Lord Marston, who had been friends with Oliver for a good many years, nodded, smiled, and shrugged. "But of course," he said calmly. "But if you do decide to do something worth betting on, you will inform me, will you not?"

Oliver sighed inwardly but nodded. "Of course."

"Capital!" Lord Marston boomed, turning back towards the other guests, watching them with a sharp eye. "Although this does make me wonder whether or not you are considering matrimony?"

Before he could prevent himself, a harsh bark of laughter ripped from Oliver's throat, making Lord Marston chuckle.

"No, indeed not!" Oliver spluttered, thinking even the idea itself was frightening. "No, I have no intention of marrying, Lord Marston. I cannot think of anything worse!"

Lord Marston chuckled, lifting his glass of whisky in a half toast. "I quite agree," he answered, gesturing to the filled ballroom with his other hand. "For then one would not be free to dance with, converse with, and acquaint oneself with the many lovely creatures here this evening." He bowed his head as a young lady drew near him. "If you will excuse me. I believe I am engaged for this dance." Handing a nearby footman his glass, Lord Marston stepped away from Oliver and took the arm of the young lady, who blushed furiously at his attention. Rolling his eyes and thinking Lord Marston himself was more than able to capture the attention of any lady he desired, Oliver retreated a few steps further back, hiding himself away in the shadows.

This was not his usual haunt, of course, but he found himself wanting to retreat from society for a short time before throwing himself headlong into it once more. Last season had been enjoyable, of course, but he had not liked being the center of attention. It had made certain ladies a little wary of him, making them unwilling to draw near to him when he had made his intentions towards them quite clear. That had taken away some of his enjoyment and marred his experience a little. He did not want the same this season.

"Marriage, indeed!" he muttered to himself, throwing back the rest of his whisky and setting the glass down onto a nearby table. The idea was preposterous! Being the Earl of Montague meant he was, of course, both wealthy and very well titled, and it was expected he would find a wife and produce the heir very soon—but one thing Oliver liked to do was to defy social expectation. Besides which, he had a very sensible younger brother who had married already and had produced two very healthy children in the space of two years. If the worst happened, then the title would go to someone who was, Oliver considered, a good deal more worthy of it than he. Therefore, he was quite determined he would not marry in the near future, for he more than enjoyed his life just as it was. It was unnecessary to complicate it with courtship, engagement, and marriage at this present time, even if Oliver fully intended to live as he pleased whether he took a wife or not! It was nothing more than a social obligation, which he would fulfill at some point, of course, but for the time being, there was no requirement to do so.

Sighing heavily, Oliver leaned back against the wall and took in the scene before him. Lord Marston's ball was one of the very first of the season every year and was certainly a very grand affair. In fact, this year seemed to be especially ambitious, given the decorations and the fact that Lord Marston was not serving cheap ratafia but what appeared to be quite excellent wine and champagne —as well as whisky and brandy for the gentlemen in the card room where Oliver had been only a few minutes earlier. Lord Marston might only be a viscount, but he had a wealth Oliver knew was equal to his own. The rest of society knew that also, which was why they always seemed so eager to have Lord Marston in their acquaintance. No doubt the gentleman would have many young ladies pressed towards him this evening, which he would take great pleasure in. Oliver allowed himself a wry smile. In that, at least, both he and Lord Marston were very similar indeed. They both appreciated the sweetness of a lady's company without having any intention of furthering the acquaintance into something more substantial. Neither of them wished to marry, and so, neither of them would even consider it at the present time. There was far too much to be enjoyed.

"Oh, Lord Montague!"

He felt someone fall into him and immediately drew himself up, pushing himself away from the wall and feeling heat climb into his face.

"I did not see you there," the lady continued, betraying herself by the fact that she had addressed him by his correct title. "I must ask what it is you are doing hiding yourself in the shadows when the ball is already underway! Surely it cannot be that you are not dancing this evening?"

Oliver cleared his throat, trying to regain his composure. "Ah, Lady Dalton," he murmured, recognizing the lady from last season and knowing full well she had not one, but two daughters who were as yet unmarried. "You find me in a moment of reflection, that is all."

The lady's eyes lit up and, as if they knew this was their moment to step forward, both of Lady Dalton's daughters appeared beside her. They were tall and somewhat gangly, with large eyes and overly long mouths. They were not twins but were less than a year apart in age, with an appearance very similar to each other. Neither was particularly beautiful but nor were they plain. Oliver still had no interest in either, despite the eagerness in Lady Dalton's eyes.

"Then I must hope your moment of reflection is past and you are able now to step forward into what is certain to be a most enjoyable evening," Lady Dalton said briskly, gesturing to her daughters. "Both Sarah and Isabella have a space or two on their dance card."

Sighing inwardly, Oliver gave both young ladies a smile—which they both returned at once. There was no easy way to extricate himself from this particular situation, it seemed, for Lady Dalton was quite determined, and he certainly could not refuse to dance with her daughters given he had every intention of doing precisely that with other, more beautiful young ladies that might capture his interest.

"But of course," he murmured, stepping forward and seeing the first young lady hand him her dance card. The steely look in her eyes matched that of her mother, but Oliver could not tell nor recall whether this one was Isabella or Sarah. Quickly, he wrote his name down for the cotillion for one and then the country dance for the other. Smiling briefly, he nodded to them both, trying desperately to remember how they were addressed.

"I thank you both," he murmured, inclining his head. "I look forward to our dances, Miss..."

Lady Dalton blinked, her brows lowering. "Miss Isabella Riley and Miss Sarah Riley," she said sharply, making him flush with embarrassment. "I know you have a great many acquaintances, Lord Montague, but I had hoped there would be *some* young ladies that you might remember."

He bowed quickly in an attempt to cover his embarrassment and to fumble around for some excuse. The last thing he wanted was for Lady Dalton to speak badly about him to her friends, for rumors of that kind were not at all welcome. "I think you will recall, Lady Dalton, I was having a moment of contemplation when you first found me. That fog of contemplation has not quite lifted from my mind as yet, I fear." This, accompanied with a somewhat apologetic looking smile, seemed to loosen the lines of irritation on Lady Dalton's face, for she sighed quietly, lifted her chin and then, eventually, gave him a small smile.

"I quite understand," she said, putting a hand on his arm that Oliver immediately wanted to shake off. "The return to society can be a difficult one, but I am quite certain there are many here who will be glad to see you."

He nodded and forced himself to smile. "You are very kind and *most* understanding," he told her, making her smile all the more. "I thank you, Lady Dalton." Excusing himself, Oliver stepped away and continued quickly into the fray, wanting to escape from Lady Dalton's clutches just as quickly as he could. That was very frustrating indeed. His behavior, it seemed, did not matter to the beau monde. He might seduce as many rich widows as he wanted, might steal kisses from otherwise innocent debu-tantes, but *still,* mothers would approach him in an attempt to push their daughters forward.

It was, of course, because they knew he would have to marry someday, and each seemed to hope their daughter would be the one to catch his eye and make him turn from his ways. Besides which, anyone could turn a blind eye to a rich and titled gentleman's foibles, given they would have the accolade of having their daughter tied to his name!

It was, he considered, all rather sordid. He would much prefer a lady keep her daughters well away from him, rejecting his wealth and title entirely, given what they knew of his character. To have so many young ladies pushed towards him made him think their mothers did not truly care about their daughters in any way whatsoever.

"Oh, do excuse me!"

He had not looked where he was going, he realized and had now walked directly into a young lady who was standing by another lady, who had immediately narrowed her gaze towards him.

"I apologize," he said at once, reaching out to take the lady's arm in case she was to stumble. Had he stood on her toes? Or merely knocked into her? "I was not looking where I was going."

"No, indeed you were not!" said the fair-haired lady, who was older than the first and was, apparently, either her mother or her companion—although given the difference in their appearance, he would think it was her companion. "Striding forward like that when there are a good many others milling about! You are much too—"

"I am quite certain it was an accident only," came the voice of the first lady, soft and quiet, in stark contrast to the sharp, angry tones of the second. "Do excuse me, my lord." Inclining her head, she made to turn away from him, forcing Oliver to let go of her arm.

He watched her for a moment or two, horrified to see she was now limping rather badly. Clearly, he had hurt her a good deal more than she was willing to say! He was a rogue, yes, and certainly a bit of a rascal, but he was not about to let a young lady walk away from him without assistance, especially not if he had been the one to hurt her so.

"I have pained you, I can see," he stammered, hurrying forward and catching the lady's arm. "Here, please do allow me to lead you to a chair where you might rest and recover."

Much to his surprise, the young lady did not immediately smile and thank him for his help. Nor did she admit that, yes, he had pained her in some way or another. Instead, she merely looked up at him for a time, her green eyes shifting from one part of his face to another as though she were trying to work out what to say to him. Her lips pressed hard together, her dark tresses pulled back from her face save from a few spiraling curls by her temples. Had Oliver not been so confused by the strange reaction to his offer of help, he would have allowed himself to consider her in a much more promising light.

"If you would let go of my arm, my lord, I would be most grateful."

Taken aback by this request, Oliver hesitated for a moment, only to let go of her arm, which dropped back to her side at once.

"Might I inquire as to your name?" she asked, her chin lifting as she looked up into his eyes. "We are not acquainted, as you might already be aware."

Clearing his throat, Oliver inclined his head, feeling a sense of embarrassment climb up his spine, although he did not know as to why. "But of course. I am the Earl of Montague," he said, looking curiously back at this young lady and wondering why she had refused his offer of help when almost every other lady of his acquaintance would not even have considered refusing it. "And you?"

Not even a flicker of a smile crossed the young lady's face. She said nothing, glancing towards her companion, who gave a tiny nod.

"This is Lady Amelia," the fair-haired lady said, gesturing towards the young lady, who did not move nor smile. "Only daughter to the late Earl of Stockbridge and now under the care of her uncle, who has taken on the title."

Oliver's ears pricked up at once. He had met the Earl of Stockbridge on one or two occasions before, given he was an Earl and had taken time for both business and pleasure in London as so many of the rich, titled gentlemen did, but he had not known he had a niece to take care of!

"And I am Mrs. Peters," the lady finished, her gaze steady and a little grim. "Companion to Lady Amelia."

"I am very glad to make your acquaintance," he said with as much charm as he could muster. "But I must insist you permit me to take you to a seat so that you might rest, especially after what I have done."

Lady Amelia blinked, paled just a little, and then regarded him carefully. "You have done nothing, Lord Montague," she stated, confusing him all the more. "But I thank you for your concern and wish you a pleasant evening." Saying nothing more, she turned away from him at once and began to walk again with her companion.

It was only in watching her that Oliver realized what Lady Amelia had meant. The limp was there again, as pronounced as ever, but not of his doing. His embarrassment flared all over again, making him realize he had done nothing to hurt the young lady as he had first thought but that this was something that had already occurred some time ago. He was not to blame, then.

"I see you have met the young Lady Amelia," said a voice in his ear. Turning, he saw Lord Marston standing there, a young lady on his arm and a broad smile on his face. "I have to invite her, of course, given her uncle's title as well as her standing in society, but I fear she will have no enjoyment from this evening."

"How could she?" the young lady on Lord Marston's arm asked, shaking her head pityingly, although her eyes were sharp as she watched Lady Amelia walk through the crowd. "What a shame. It would be better for her if she had remained at home. No one is going to be interested in her, of course."

"Of course," Oliver found himself saying, as Lord Marston shrugged, throwing aside the matter quickly.

"You must find your partner for the cotillion, which is due to begin in a moment," Lord Marston stated as Oliver turned his head away from watching Lady Amelia. "Do tell me you have someone, Montague?"

Oliver shrugged, sighed, and rolled his eyes. "Unfortunately, I do," he muttered, thinking of the uninteresting Miss Riley. "I must go in search of her."

"Indeed you must," Lord Marston grinned, looking into the young lady's eyes and patting her hand. "For this is only the start of the season, and we must make the most of it!"

"You are quite right," Oliver agreed, pushing away the last traces of embarrassment that clung to him as he thought of Lady Amelia. "I should go and find Miss Riley, and thereafter, I shall secure the rest of my dances for this evening."

"Just not with Lady Amelia," the young lady said, her voice heavy with mirth. Lord Marston laughed aloud and pulled his companion towards the dance floor, leaving Oliver with a slightly heavy sensation in his heart that he could not quite explain.

Putting it down to the realization that he was first to dance with Miss Riley and had not yet found any other suitable partners for the remaining dances, other than her sister, Oliver set his shoulders and began to search for Miss Riley. Lord Marston was quite right. This evening was to be enjoyed, and Oliver was quite determined to do just that.

CHAPTER THREE

$\mathcal{T}$he first week of the season dragged by. Amelia found each engagement to be more trying than the last for, as the *ton* grew more aware of her presence, she found herself to be the object of their attention whenever she even stepped into a room. Mrs. Peters had, of course, been as firm and as determined as ever before, helping Amelia through the muddy waters that surrounded her and giving her more courage to remain steadfast in her resolution not to allow the *ton*'s whispers to affect her outwardly.

Inwardly was quite another matter. Amelia could already feel the weight of their disdain on her shoulders, knowing they did not think her suitable to be a part of the *ton*. They did not allow imperfection. Such things were pushed from society one way or the other—just as she would be in the end. Their whispers, their gossiping, and their laughter would bite at her until she finally turned away, unable to take any more of their mockery.

"Ah, Amelia."

Amelia turned away from the window at once, blinking back tears and seeing Mrs. Peters coming towards her, a small smile on her face.

"You must get ready at once," she said, not saying a word about Amelia's current lack of composure. "We are to call upon a lady I met only yesterday."

Amelia blinked, steadying herself just a little. "A new acquaintance?"

"Indeed," Mrs. Peters replied with a quick smile. "I heard of her from another companion, who heard about her from...well, I do not know where, and I have decided you must meet with her at once."

"I see," Amelia murmured, not entirely understanding what her companion meant. "And why must I do so?"

At this, Mrs. Peters beamed at Amelia, her face lighting up. "Because this lady is not only rich, titled, and has standing in society, but she also has a willingness of spirit that speaks of kindness and compassion. I am certain she will be more than happy to aid you in the same way as she has agreed to with two other young ladies."

There was very little in this short explanation that Amelia understood. In fact, she was so puzzled that for a few moments, she did nothing other than look at Mrs. Peters, waiting for her to explain herself further. When Mrs. Peters did not, Amelia let out a long, heavy sigh and shook her head.

"Very well," she said with a small shrug. "I presume the lady is expecting me?"

"She is," Mrs. Peters replied quickly, gesturing for

Amelia to walk towards the door. "I was bold and intro-duced myself to her at the soiree last evening."

Amelia gaped at her companion, not moving an inch. "Why would you do something so improper?" she asked hoarsely, her heart beginning to beat frantically. "The lady will think I am very rude, indeed!"

Mrs. Peters shrugged, reached out, and grasped Amelia's arm gently. "I do not think she will," she replied, beginning to guide Amelia towards the door. "She seemed quite understanding, and when I explained why I wished to set up a short introduction, I must say, Lady Smithton seemed to understand at once, even if she was a little surprised."

Amelia wanted to groan aloud, not quite certain what had taken place but fearing her companion had over-stepped in one way or another. She knew nothing of this lady but feared, already, there would be a bad impression of Amelia and her present circumstances.

"She will not think ill of you nor look down upon you," Mrs. Peters said reassuringly. "She is very kind indeed and has had trials of her own. Her husband passed away when they were not long married, although his death has left her very wealthy and, as such, entirely independent."

Amelia shook her head in disbelief, looking up at the staircase and groaning inwardly at the challenge that lay before her. Having to climb them to reach her bedchamber was one of the few things that truly irked her. She had asked her uncle to consider moving one of the bedchambers below stairs to help her with her limp, but he had steadfastly refused. Thus, she always had to climb them when the occasion required her to change, as it did today. Gripping the handrail with one hand, she clutched at it tightly before hauling her body up the stairs one at a time, trying not to put weight on her painful leg. If she did so, then a shooting agony would course up through her, making her catch her breath and wince. Her leg had never been the same since the day she had fallen from that tree all those years ago, and Amelia did not think it would ever improve. Her pain came daily and was something she had been forced to come to accept.

"Lady Smithton has, from what I understand, become willing to help two young ladies who have very few prospects and who will soon be considered too old to marry," Mrs. Peters continued, walking slowly beside Amelia and not hurrying her in any way. "I am quite certain she will be able to help you also if you ask it of her."

"Help me?" Amelia muttered, sweat beading on her brow as she tried to hurry forward. "What do you mean, Mrs. Peters?" She gritted her teeth and continued to make her way up the final few steps, desperate for the relief that would come when she reached the very top.

Mrs. Peters waved a hand, knowing all too well that Amelia did not want her help when it came to the staircase but remaining by her side regardless. "I do not know precisely what she will do," she said with a quick shrug. "But it will be of greater help to you than I can be at this moment, I am certain of that. After all, she was wife to a Marquess, whereas I am nothing but a mere companion!"

Swallowing hard, Amelia held back her worries and fears, keeping them hidden behind her lips. She could not understand why the rich widow of a Marquess would wish to have any involvement with someone such as herself, but it seemed Mrs. Peters was quite confident that the lady was more than willing. It did not make particular sense to Amelia herself, but if there was to be even a flicker of hope she would make a success of this season, then did she not have to take every opportunity presented to her? Did she not have to try her utmost to do whatever she could so that she would not fail entirely?

"You have nothing to fear," Mrs. Peters murmured as they walked together into Amelia's bedchamber, with Amelia needing to sit down at once so that her leg would give her a little relief. "Lady Smithton is shrewd but kind. I know she will be willing to listen to everything you have to say—and you must tell her everything."

"Everything?" Amelia repeated as Mrs. Peters walked to the wardrobe and threw back the doors, clearly searching for something that would be both appropriate and elegant for Amelia to wear. "What can you mean?"

Mrs. Peters' voice reached her, a little muffled, as she thrust her head further inside the wardrobe. "You know very well what I mean, Amelia! You tell her about your father's illness, your uncle taking on the title and the responsibility for you, about the dictate by him that you must find a suitor by the end of the season, *and* about your limp and how society treats you because of it. You must tell her of your hopes, your wishes for the future, as well as your fears. Tell her everything, Amelia, and tell her the truth. Only then will she be able to see you are truly in need of her help."

~

Almost two hours later, Amelia found herself ushered into a very grand drawing room. It had beautiful furnishings that caught her eye everywhere she looked, with delicate touches that spoke of elegance and refinement. It appeared Mrs. Peters had been quite correct in her judgment that Lady Smithton was substantially wealthy!

"Ah, Lady Amelia," came a kind voice, and Amelia turned to see a tall, youthful-looking lady walking towards her from the other end of the room. "And Mrs. Peters. How glad I am to see you both."

Amelia dipped into a curtsy as best she could; her leg paining her, but she forced herself to do it anyway. "Thank you for agreeing to see me," she stammered, not quite certain what else to say. "I will admit this has come as something of a surprise."

Lady Smithton laughed and threw Mrs. Peters a glance. "Your companion was very persuasive indeed," she answered, which made Mrs. Peters flush just a little. "Although I am very glad to make your acquaintance, Lady Amelia. Please, do sit down." She gestured towards three chairs cloistered close towards a small fireplace, which was empty, with a carved stand set in front of it for decoration. "And I shall have refreshments sent in at once."

Amelia, grateful to sit down, moved as quickly as she could, feeling her shame begin to creep up out of her soul all over again with the awareness that Lady Smithton could see her limp very clearly.

"Pray, do not be embarrassed," Lady Smithton

murmured, surprising Amelia with her awareness of what was going on in Amelia's heart. "You have nothing to fear from me, Lady Amelia. I will not shame you nor whisper about you nor spread rumors or gossip, as I am certain so many others have done before."

Amelia sank into a chair, waiting for Lady Smithton to do so also before she spoke. A quick glance towards Mrs. Peters confirmed the lady was expecting her to speak honestly, as she had been encouraged to do only a short time before.

"I—I am grateful for that, Lady Smithton," she said, looking back at the lady and seeing the smile on her face that reached to her eyes. "You are quite right to suggest the *ton* are less than willing to overlook my limp. Their whispers grow quite overwhelming at times."

Lady Smithton nodded, the smile fading from her face and being slowly replaced by a look of displeasure. "I quite understand," she stated, firmly. "I have had a great many rumors chasing after me since my return to society —mostly surrounding the reasons behind my husband's death, which some might like to implicate me in—so I well understand your struggle, Lady Amelia. You can have complete confidence in me. I shall not treat you as the beau monde have done."

"I am delighted to hear it," Amelia replied fervently. "I am short of understanding and compassionate acquaintances, Lady Smithton, so this has come as a very great relief."

"But of course." Lady Smithton made to say more but was prevented by the maids entering the room with trays stacked high with various delicacies. Amelia was astonished by the sheer amount presented, whilst Mrs. Peters began to smile in wonder.

"Please, help yourself and allow me to pour the tea," Lady Smithton said, waving a hand towards the many different cakes, small pastries, and other treats. "And do not feel you need to fulfill any sort of propriety. I find I am vastly hungry around this time in the afternoon, and there is still a good length of time until I am to dine again!"

Amelia, seeing how Mrs. Peters did as Lady Smithton asked, took only a moment or two to follow suit, shooting a quick glance towards Lady Smithton out of the corner of her eye and thinking she was, in fact, quite different to any lady of quality she had met before. Perhaps there was a way for Lady Smithton to help her in her desire to find a suitor.

"Now," Lady Smithton said once the tea had been served. "Mrs. Peters has become aware that I have offered to aid two young ladies who are nearing spinsterhood." She gave Mrs. Peters a quick smile, a slightly teasing note in her voice. "Although quite how she has heard such a thing, I cannot say!"

Mrs. Peters did not look in the least abashed, saying nothing but smiling broadly.

"Therefore, I believe she hopes I can aid you in a similar fashion, Lady Amelia," Lady Smithton continued without hesitation. "I presume your difficulties come from being seen only for your limp?"

There was not even a momentary pause as she spoke of Amelia's limp. That was, Amelia decided, fairly refreshing, for Lady Smithton spoke forthrightly and did not once refrain from speaking of what might be seen as a delicate matter.

"I fell out of a tree when I was twelve years old," she began by way of explanation. "My leg has never been the same. It is my own doing, I suppose, although—"

"I would not hold such a thing against you!" Lady Smithton interrupted, in evident surprise. "And nor would I be unwilling to help you because of it."

Amelia smiled, feeling more and more encouraged. "I am very glad for your kindness," she said quietly. "For not everyone sees the occasion of my accident as you do." Pausing so that she might push back her sudden flood of tears, which had come from the simple kindness shown by Lady Smithton, Amelia drew in a long breath. "My uncle has taken on the title once carried by my father. I was late to the season given first my father's illness and then my year of mourning. Last season was my debut, but it did not go particularly well, and no gentleman showed me any interest whatsoever—much to my uncle's dismay. I must now find a suitor this year, but I cannot think there will be any more success this year than I had at the last. I am not changed in any way; my limp has not improved, and the *ton* is all the more eager to point out my struggles to anyone they can. Gentlemen do nothing but tease me, and not once have I been asked to dance." A faint blush crept into her cheeks at the questioning look in Lady Smithton's eyes. "I can dance some of the dances, Lady Smithton, but only if they are slow and do not require a great many steps."

"And we are always concerned a gentleman's feet might be heavy and could step on Lady Amelia's foot, making her pain all the worse," Mrs. Peters interjected, as Lady Smithton nodded in understanding. "But the beau monde appears to believe she is quite useless when it comes to dancing."

Amelia's face clouded at the truths that came from Mrs. Peters' lips. It was just as she said, but still, the pain of it struck her heart, hard. "Do you think there is any hope, Lady Smithton?" she asked, fearing this would all come to naught. "Or am I to resign myself to my fate?"

Lady Smithton frowned. "You have no need to even *consider* the idea that there is no hope, Lady Amelia," she stated, making Amelia's heart flare with furious hope. "There are plenty of gentlemen who care nothing for such things and who have no intention of behaving as arrogantly or as callously as the gentlemen you have met thus far!" She sighed heavily and shook her head. "It displeases me there are so many gentlemen and ladies who behave in such an uncouth and uncivil manner. For whatever reason, they appear to flock together and grow in number when even a small matter of interest reaches their ears."

"I could not agree more," Mrs. Peters said, looking at Amelia with a hardness about her eyes that betrayed her dislike of the *ton*. "Lady Amelia has endured a great deal, and I have been seeking some way to encourage her." She turned her attention back to Lady Smithton. "Are you able to help us further, Lady Smithton? Lady Amelia has no one to turn to, for both her parents are gone from this earth, and her uncle does not care to involve himself as he ought. I have done my best, but it is very little in comparison to what someone with such strong standing in society might do."

Amelia felt herself blush, knowing Mrs. Peters was speaking very openly indeed, stating matters with such certainty that Amelia felt a little exposed. Daring a glance at Lady Smithton, she saw the lady look back at her steadily, her expression quite calm.

"But of course," Lady Smithton said as Amelia lowered her gaze to the floor, now entirely overwhelmed by the lady's kindness. "I will ensure you are introduced to gentlemen worthy of you, Lady Amelia. Without wishing to appear proud, I am quite certain no one will dare whisper about you within my hearing. In addition, my friend Lord Havisham will also assist."

Amelia swallowed the lump in her throat, but it did not dislodge itself. Tears began to pool in her eyes, and she blinked hastily, not wanting to lose her composure in front of the lady, but she could not prevent one from slipping out and running down her cheek.

"Oh, do excuse me," she murmured, embarrassed. "I did not mean to—"

"There is nothing to apologize for," Lady Smithton said quietly. "You have endured a great deal thus far, Lady Amelia. I quite understand that. But you will no longer have to struggle. There is friendship here, waiting for you. I shall introduce you to the other young ladies, and you will see there is a kinship between you all that will both encourage and strengthen you. You will find you are no longer alone in your suffering." She smiled and leaned forward in her chair, her eyes filled with a hope Amelia clung to. "And you will discover, Lady

Amelia, that soirees, balls, dinners, and the like are no longer something to dread but rather something to enjoy. With friends, acquaintances, and welcoming smiles, you will begin to feel a part of society in a way you have not before. You must ignore the whispers, set aside those who seek to mock you, for they are of no value. Instead, focus on those who see you as you truly are and who will not have a single word of gossip on their tongues." Her smile broadened, and she sat back in her chair. "There are plenty of them, Lady Amelia, and I will be very glad indeed to introduce them to you."

Amelia pulled out a lace handkerchief and wiped at her eyes, her heart filled with a desperate hope that flared light and heat all through her. "Thank you, Lady Smithton," she said hoarsely, seeing how Mrs. Peters was also attempting to regain her composure. "You are kindness itself."

Lady Smithton waved a hand dismissively. "Come now," she said, a little more decisively. "We must begin to consider your next social occasion so that I might make it quite plain to the *ton* that you and I are now well acquainted." Throwing a quick smile to Mrs. Peters, Lady Smithton spread out her hands. "What is it you are to attend next?"

Amelia allowed Mrs. Peters to explain, knowing she was the one who knew such things better than she did herself! Sitting back in her chair with her lace handkerchief screwed up into a ball in one hand, Amelia allowed herself to relax just a little, letting out a long breath and feeling a sense of happiness begin to climb into her heart. It washed over her, giving her a sense of warmth that enveloped her completely. She was no longer to be alone in her suffering. She would have acquaintances who understood her struggles and might even make a friend of Lady Smithton.

Finally, there was a hope that this season would not come to naught and that, instead, it might prove itself to be the happiest year of her life.

CHAPTER FOUR

Oliver sighed inwardly as he plastered a smile on his face and walked into Lord Burton's drawing-room. There was to be a soiree this evening, with cards, music and good conversation, but Oliver was not at all inclined to be present. His head ached from a little too much brandy the previous evening and even having a few hours to rest earlier in the day had not brought him much relief.

But he had accepted the invitation and knew he could not refuse to appear, especially when he had every intention of making his way to Whites later on. Lord Burton would consider it an affront if Oliver were to do such a thing and no doubt, there would be some consequences to deal with thereafter.

"Ah, Lord Montague!"

His smile still fixed firmly to his face, Oliver bowed in greeting, murmuring a word of thanks towards Lord and Lady Burton, who both thanked him in return for attending.

"There are many lovely young ladies here this evening, Lord Montague," Lord Burton said, stepping away from his wife and speaking a little conspiratorially. "My wife has done so deliberately, choosing those who are less inclined towards making a particularly strong appearance at society events for one reason or another." He shrugged, looking a little embarrassed. "My wife has a kind heart, and I could not refuse her this."

"Of course not," Oliver muttered, thinking this evening would be even duller than he had first anticipated. "That is kind indeed of Lady Burton to think of such...people."

Lord Burton nodded, with something flaring in his eyes that Oliver did not quite understand. He watched with interest as Lord Burton glanced back at his wife before returning his attention to Oliver. Was it that the fellow had come to feel a fondness for his wife? That was most unexpected if it were the case, for Lord Burton had not wanted to marry. This time last season, he was doing all he could to remove himself from an engagement he did not want but which had been in place since he himself had been a young boy. Now, it seemed, there was something significantly different about the way he looked at his wife.

"My wife has a very considerate heart," Lord Burton said, his smile softening his eyes all the more. "I have found her to be kindness itself, I confess."

Oliver blinked, a little unsure as to what to say to this remark. He had never felt anything other than unbridled desire for the young ladies or widows he pursued, and therefore had no understanding of what Lord Burton was apparently feeling.

"It was very foolish of me to fight against our marriage in the way I did," Lord Burton finished with a broad smile in Oliver's direction. "It is my hope, therefore, that this evening, you might find yourself looking at the young ladies without any of your dark intentions."

Oliver frowned at this, feeling a little needled by the remark. "I do not understand what you mean, Lord Burton," he said, a little more sharply than he had meant. "Dark intentions?"

Lord Burton chuckled and slapped Oliver on the shoulder, making Oliver want to recoil as far away from the man as possible. He said nothing more but waited for Lord Burton to explain himself as his anger continued to burn a little more hotly with every second that passed.

"My dear fellow," Lord Burton said eventually in a rather booming voice that made Oliver wince. "The *ton* knows very well you are not a gentleman who wishes to court without having any particular intention towards them other than to satisfy your desires." He lifted one brow in silent challenge, and Oliver found he could not easily contradict the gentleman, given everything he had said thus far was quite true. "That is why I speak of 'dark intentions,' Lord Montague. Your intentions are not considered to be gentlemanly, and I must insist you give no attention to such plans this evening." His voice became sterner as he turned just a little to face Oliver more directly. "Why do you not see if there are any ladies here who might just capture your attention in a way other than what you are used to?"

Oliver snorted in derision and turned his head away. "I do not think such a thing will be possible," he said without either hesitation or embarrassment. "I seek out the company of ladies for a specific reason and I—"

"Just for one evening," Lord Burton interrupted, holding up one hand. "Make your way around the room. Converse with each person present, instead of looking at them in a way that only speaks to your desires. See if any here are able to capture your attention in a way you have never thought possible." He chuckled, lifting one eyebrow. "Or do you think you are so very uninteresting that you will have nothing to say and they might be the ones to turn from you?"

Gritting his teeth, Oliver bit back his first, sharp response and looked around the room quickly. Lord Burton was quite correct. There *were* young ladies present whom he had never been introduced to and certainly would never have sought an introduction to either. He preferred bright, vivacious, enchanting young ladies to the quieter, dull creatures who needed a good deal of encouragement before they opened up to him even a little. But this evening, it seemed, he was going to be surrounded by such creatures and would have no choice but to speak to them in the way Lord Burton suggested.

"I am quite certain I will be able to make pleasant conversation if that is what you are asking me to do," he muttered as Lord Burton slapped him on the shoulder again, making him grit his teeth in frustration. "And I shall be able to do it very well indeed."

"You shall have to lose all of your usual charms," Lord

Burton laughed as he turned away. "For none here will react to it in the way you are used to." And, so saying, he turned away from Oliver and moved back to stand by his wife, ready to greet the rest of his guests.

Oliver sighed heavily, looking at the other guests and allowing his gaze to rest on each one for just a short moment. He did not know very many of them at all, although one or two he recognized. They were not overly pretty nor confident in their manner, which needled him. Perhaps he should have found an excuse not to attend this evening, given the dullness that lay before him.

"Good evening, Lord Burton."

A voice he recognized caught his ears as he glanced behind him, seeing a young lady step into the room with a fair-haired companion just behind her. His stomach dropped to the floor, and his heart began to quicken with embarrassment as he recognized the young lady whom he had thought he had injured, only to realize she had a bad limp. Turning his head away, he winced as he heard Lord Burton's booming voice reach his ears.

"And might I present, whilst I have the opportunity, the Earl of Montague to you, Lady Amelia?"

Clearing his throat and having no other choice but to do as Lord Burton now insisted, Oliver turned around and inclined his head towards the young lady, trying desperately to prevent the flare of heat he felt in his chest from rising to his face. "Lady Amelia," he said, lifting his head and sending any angry glance towards Lord Burton, who was now grinning broadly. "How very good to see you again."

"Ah!" Lord Burton exclaimed, one hand on his heart

as he looked from Lady Amelia to Oliver and back again. "You are already acquainted. Wonderful, quite wonderful." He bowed hastily and took his leave, returning to his position beside his wife as the last few guests began to come into the room.

"You remember Mrs. Peters," Lady Amelia said quietly, glancing to her left and gesturing to the smaller, fair-haired lady. "She is my companion."

"But of course," Oliver said smoothly, bowing to Mrs. Peters and silently thinking to himself that this evening would not get any better. "How are you, Mrs. Peters?"

"Very well," Mrs. Peters replied with a tight smile. "Thank you, Lord Montague."

He managed to smile but then could not think of anything more to say. There was still embarrassment that rose up within him when he thought of what had occurred previously between himself and Lady Amelia. Looking about him, he cleared his throat and then tried to find even the smallest, most innocuous remark with which to break the silence.

"I—I do hope you enjoyed the ball, Lady Amelia."

Cringing inwardly as he said those words, Oliver looked at Lady Amelia and forced himself to smile, knowing their previous meeting was the only thing he ought not to have mentioned.

"The ball?" Lady Amelia looked back at him, her green eyes more vivid than he remembered them. In fact, the more he looked at her, the more Oliver began to realize just how pretty the young lady was. She had a delicate oval face, with dark tresses that allowed a few wisps about her temples whilst the rest were held back.

Oliver found himself musing as to just how long Lady Amelia's hair might be, allowing his gaze to drift down her gentle curves and wondering if she might be a rather easy conquest. She would not be captured by any other gentleman, given her limp, which meant she might be quite willing to step into his arms and allow him to steal a few kisses. He would do nothing more, of course, for he did not treat innocent creatures such as she in that way, but it would be interesting to see if she would permit his attentions.

"Lord Montague?"

There was a hardness to Lady Amelia's voice that jerked him back to the present, making him realize that not only had he not answered her as yet, but he had also spent the last few moments in silent contemplation, thinking of things he ought not to have been.

"I apologize," he said, bowing quickly as a flush crept up his neck. "I should not have mentioned the ball. I did not mean to upset you."

"You did not."

He blinked in surprise, taken aback by the sharpness to her voice and even more astonished at the dark expression that now captured her features. She had not appeared thus when he had first met her at the ball, thinking she was nothing more than a poor creature who wanted to hide herself away from his—and society's —view.

"I have a limp," she declared, making him take a small step back such was the fervor with which she spoke. "That is all, Lord Montague. There is nothing for me to be ashamed of and, indeed, I will no longer permit myself to be made to feel as though it is something I ought to hide away." She lifted her chin, and Oliver noticed a shard of determination in her eyes, which he had not noticed before. "Do not think our prior meeting brought me any shame, Lord Montague," she finished, her head held high, and her expression radiating boldness. "For I can assure you, I feel no such thing."

For some moments, Oliver could not quite find a response. Lady Amelia was speaking in a way he had not expected, and he did not quite know what he ought to say nor how he ought to act. He managed a small smile, inclining his head towards her as he fought to find something appropriate to say. "But of course," he said, cringing just a little at his lack of response. "I did not mean to... what I should say is—"

"Lady Amelia, you have arrived!"

Oliver looked up, relieved he was no longer going to have to struggle to find something to say. An elegant lady approached, her eyes bright, and her hand outstretched towards Lady Amelia. He recognized her at once. This was none other than Lady Smithton, who had dealt with a good deal of rumor and the like herself, given people liked to whisper about the death of her late husband and considered that Lady Smithton might have had something to do with it. Lady Smithton had shown no sign of being affected by the gossip, which he had admired. At one point, Oliver had considered approaching Lady Smithton himself, given she was a wealthy, independent widow who might wish for a little more intimate company with a gentleman of her acquaintance, but in the end, he had chosen to stay away from her. Lady

Smithton was a little too confident and a little too determined for his liking. He much preferred ladies who were a bit quieter.

"How very good to see you," Lady Amelia murmured, greeting Lady Smithton. "Do you know the Earl of Montague?" Lady Amelia glanced towards Oliver, her eyes barely landing on him before she turned her head away again. "He and I have been recently acquainted."

Lady Smithton curtsied quickly, just as Oliver bowed, murmuring a greeting.

"Yes," Lady Smithton replied, speaking only to Lady Amelia. "Yes, I am acquainted with Lord Montague." She gave him another sharp glance, clearly well aware of his reputation. "You must excuse us, Lord Montague. I have a few people I wish to introduce Lady Amelia to."

"But of course," he murmured, realizing Lady Smithton was trying to extract Lady Amelia from his company and finding himself a little irritated by it. Lady Amelia inclined her head in farewell, whilst Mrs. Peters did not even glance at him before following after her charge. Oliver was left standing alone, his temper flaring hot within him as embarrassment poured into his heart. Lady Smithton did not want him near Lady Amelia, and Lady Amelia herself was clearly willing to do as Lady Smithton asked. That was to be expected, he supposed, given Lady Smithton was more than able to encourage and support Lady Amelia within society, but still, her actions grated at him. The anger within him made him want to pursue Lady Amelia all the more, to make her fall in love with him so that he might steal her kisses and draw her close to him, only to then separate themselves completely and move onto another. It was a desire born from anger, from frustration and from the shame that now nudged at his heart, rather than his usual consideration that she was pretty and much too innocent to be ignored.

"What did you say to her?"

"I said nothing," Oliver muttered, turning towards Lord Burton and wishing that the gentleman would leave him alone. "I was merely making conversation."

"Rather poor conversation, it seems," Lord Burton muttered, gesturing towards Lord Havisham, who was now being introduced to Lady Amelia by Lady Smithton. "Lord Havisham seems to be much better company in the eyes of Lady Smithton."

"I am sure he is," Oliver replied, forcing his frustration down. "You know very well it is unwise for ladies to allow their charges near me, Lord Burton." He shrugged, trying to brush off any more embarrassment that he had been left standing alone whilst Lady Smithton took Lady Amelia away from him. "Therefore, it is quite understandable for Lady Smithton to behave in such a way. I applaud her sense."

Lord Burton said nothing but studied Oliver in a way Oliver felt to be most uncomfortable. It was as though Lord Burton did not believe him and was now waiting for him to speak truthfully. Oliver kept his mouth shut tight, feeling a good deal of awkwardness but refusing to say another word.

"I do hope you have better success during the rest of the evening," Lord Burton said eventually. "The musical section is about to start, and I hope you will enjoy that also. Perhaps Lady Amelia will play for us, and you might be able to compliment her thereafter, without her companion and her friend pulling her away." He gave Oliver a broad wink, which irritated Oliver even more, before turning away and leaving Oliver to stand alone.

Wandering forward so that he would not be seen to be standing by himself all over again, Oliver grabbed a glass of brandy from one of the footmen and made his way to the shadowy corners of the room. How he wished he had made the decision to stay away from Lord Burton's gathering and had gone to Whites as he had wished! Now that he was here, he could not easily escape and leave for the gentleman's club. He would have to endure another hour or so before he might finally have the opportunity to depart. And endure he would, even if it meant staying precisely where he was and not conversing with anyone else.

CHAPTER FIVE

"*T*hat was a wonderful performance."

Oliver nodded slowly as the gentleman beside him commented on Lady Amelia's performance at the pianoforte. He had come to sit down with the rest of the guests so that they might pay rapt attention to those who came to either play or sing for the gathered crowd, wondering just how long he might have to stay before he could leave altogether.

And then, Lady Amelia had come to sit down by the pianoforte, and everything had changed. Her voice had captured his full attention, the gentleness of her song pushing away his frustration, his anger, and his upset, and leaving, in their place, a quiet peace he could not seem to push from himself.

"Oh, it appears she is to sing another!" said the gentleman, although this time he spoke to the gentleman beside him. "Who would have thought a cripple would be able to perform in such a way?"

Much to Oliver's surprise, a streak of anger ran

straight up his spine and sent his hands curling into fists. There was no need for him to feel any sort of anger given Lady Amelia was, as this gentleman had said, a cripple. But he had never once considered that her limp would prevent her from playing the pianoforte and singing for the audience. He heard the two gentlemen laugh darkly, hearing fragments of remarks that came from the one sitting a little further away and felt his anger beginning to burn all the more. He could not understand himself, could not explain why he felt so much anger when he himself would have made such a remark had he been in different company.

"Just a final piece," he heard someone say to Lady Amelia, looking back at her to see Lady Amelia blushing profusely, her cheeks a bright pink and her eyes darting all over the place, clearly a little awkward. "What say you to this?"

Their host, Lord Burton, beamed delightedly at Lady Amelia as she nodded, accepted the music from him and settled it in front of her. His heart lifted in expectation, his whole body tensing just a little as though he were waiting eagerly for her to bring that same peace to his heart as she had done only a few minutes before.

The first notes broke through the quiet and very soon, he was being carried away on a river of calm. His eyes closed as she continued to sing, thinking this was the most beautiful song he had ever heard. Lady Amelia's voice was gentle yet strong, merging with the piano in the most beautiful duet. He did not know what it was she was singing about, did not find he cared, but felt as though all he wanted to do was listen to her sing.

It came to an end much too soon, and Oliver began to clap in earnest, truly glad to have been present in the room for her performance. He watched her closely as Lord Burton came around to the pianoforte and offered her his arm, seeing how she accepted it gratefully. Her limp was barely noticeable as she walked alongside Lord Burton, who helped her back towards her chair beside Lady Smithton and Mrs. Peters, both of whom bent their heads to, no doubt, whisper congratulations to Lady Amelia.

"And now we have Miss Fairbank," Lord Burton exclaimed as Oliver continued to watch Lady Amelia, who was sitting to his right, meaning he could see her profile but very little else. As Miss Fairbank came to sit down at the pianoforte, Oliver felt his heart begin to sink back down into his soul, his spirits dwindling fast and returning to the frustrated anger that had been there ever since Lady Smithton had pulled Lady Amelia away.

"Are you going to take her on, Lord Montague?"

Jumping in surprise, he turned to see the gentleman next to him—one Lord Davidson—grinning at him. "I beg your pardon?"

"You are watching Lady Amelia very closely," Lord Davidson said with a wiggle of his eyebrows. "Are you considering her to be your next conquest? If so, then I shall put a bet down in Whites, in the hope of turning my fortunes around!" He chuckled, although wincing just a little. "My coffers are a little low given my lack of success in cards of late."

Oliver shook his head, remembering his steadfast determination not to do as he had done last year, where gentlemen placed bets on which young lady or widow he might turn his attention to next. "I fear I must disappoint you, Davidson," he replied with a half-smile. "I do not think I shall be drawing near to Lady Amelia."

Lord Davidson chuckled, let out a long, mocking sigh, and rolled his eyes. "I suppose I cannot blame you, given the way the lady is," he remarked, sending another flare of anger along Oliver's spine. "She is quite lovely of face, of course, but that leg..." He sighed again, trailing off whilst his eyes flicked towards Lady Amelia again. "I pity the gentleman that finds himself drawing close to her. I know she has a very large dowry—no doubt, to make up for what she lacks—but even that would not tempt me."

Oliver gritted his teeth, forcing back his anger and telling himself he had no reason to feel anything at all over Lady Amelia. It was a most unusual feeling for him, given he had never felt anything for any young lady before, especially not for someone who was a little less than perfect. That was what he sought, was it not? Perfection. A young lady who was nothing short of a diamond of the first water, entirely innocent and warned to be careful of gentlemen and their foibles. It was a game he played, slowly teasing the lady until finally, she gave in and allowed him to pull her into his embrace. When she stepped away from everything she had been told, everything she had been warned about, and gave in to his charms.

And then, the victory would be his. The conquest had been successful, and the lady was then entirely forgotten. He would leave her, refusing to pursue her any longer and certainly not tempting her any further. That was not the sort of gentleman he was. But whenever he sought out someone new, it was never anyone who lacked beauty or elegance. It certainly would not be someone who walked with a limp and brought a good deal of attention towards themselves because of it! So why, then, was he feeling such anger towards Lord Davidson due to his remarks?

The performance from Miss Fairbank came to a close and was applauded by the audience, although to Oliver's ears, it was a little less than what had been given to Lady Amelia. Rising from his chair and ignoring Lord Davidson's request that he remain so that they might discuss things further, Oliver found his feet making their way towards Lady Amelia. She too had risen from her chair—as had the rest of the guests—and was now standing next to Mrs. Peters and Lady Smithton, who were all listening to another lady's conversation—someone Oliver did not recognize. Lady Amelia's cheeks were a little flushed, and she was nodding gently, her expression one of embarrassment. Oliver thought the lady must be complimenting Lady Amelia on her performance and paused for a moment, taking in Lady Amelia's expression and wondering whether she had ever been given a compliment before.

Moving a few steps closer, he put a smile on his face as both Mrs. Peters and Lady Smithton looked at him, the smiles falling from their faces as they watched him draw near to Lady Amelia. Oliver ignored them both, focusing entirely on Lady Amelia and waiting politely until the other lady finally took her leave.

"Lady Amelia," he said, extending his hand towards

her and smiling into her eyes. "May I say that your performance this evening was quite wonderful."

Lady Amelia blinked, her hand remaining steadfastly by her side. Oliver chose to keep his extended, praying she would give him her hand so that he might bow over it.

"It was breathtaking," he continued, when she said nothing. "I wished it would never come to an end."

Mrs. Peters cleared her throat gently, and Oliver saw Lady Amelia start in surprise. Her cheeks filled with color, and she put her hand quickly into his, her touch a little hesitant as she looked away from him, clearly a little lost for words.

"I—I thank you, Lord Montague," she replied, her voice very soft indeed. "I am glad you enjoyed it."

Finally having her hand in his, Oliver made sure to bow over her hand for a few moments longer than was appropriate, his lips very near to her skin but not quite touching. Hearing her swift intake of breath and smiling to himself, he lifted his head and smiled at Lady Amelia again and finally let go of her hand.

"I hope I might hear you perform again some time soon," he said, seeing how she blushed and feeling a faint sense of triumph rising within him. "I must depart now, but I wanted to ensure you knew of my appreciation before I left."

Oliver smiled, nodded to Lady Smithton and Mrs. Peters, bowed to them both, and then turned away from the three ladies, making his way towards the door. He had left Lady Amelia with what he hoped was an excellent impression of his character, which might fly in the face of what Lady Smithton would say, but he had faced such a thing before. He had managed to encourage a lady's attention, even though her mother or companion had been less than willing.

Wait.

His mind began to whirl, forcing his steps to slow. He had no intention of capturing Lady Amelia's attention, so why was he thinking of her as though she was to be his next mark? Had what Lord Davidson said pierced his mind more than he had been aware? Or was it because he had to admit Lady Amelia was, in fact, quite beautiful?

Sighing to himself, Oliver shook his head, ran one hand through his hair, and then forcefully marched towards the door. He did not need to do anything other than make his way to Whites, order himself a drink, and forget entirely about Lady Amelia. She meant nothing to him and certainly was not worth his attention.

That being said, her singing had been exquisite. He would not deny that he thought her quite wonderful in that regard, and a part of him was glad he had been able to compliment her so. A small smile crept across his face as he thought of how she had blushed as he had bowed over her hand, to the point that he found his spirits lifting all over again.

"To Whites," he muttered, quickly walking out of the door and choosing to close his mind to any further thoughts of Lady Amelia. Perhaps he would get to hear her sing at another time during the Season, but it did not matter to him whether or not they furthered their acquaintance. He did not care about whether he would see her again, nor if they would ever get to converse further.

At least, that was what he repeatedly told himself as he stepped out into the darkness, ready to climb into his carriage. The memory of her gentle smile as she accepted his compliments continued to linger in his mind as the carriage rolled away, making it all the more difficult for him to forget about her completely. But forget about her he must, for Lady Amelia could never be a conquest for him. She was not perfect and, as such, not worth his time. Settling back into the carriage, Oliver closed his eyes and rested his head back against the squabs. Perhaps it was time to set his attention onto someone new, to start on his first conquest of the Season. Someone beautiful. Someone entirely perfect. And someone who would remove every trace of Lady Amelia from his mind.

"I thought we might find you here!"

Oliver groaned aloud as Lord Davidson wandered into the room, pointing a long finger in Oliver's direction.

"You left Lord Burton's very quickly indeed," Lord Davidson said in a slightly accusing tone. "It is not because you wanted to hide from us, was it?"

"No," Oliver replied stoutly, a little bit more embold-ened with a good deal of brandy now running through his veins. "I did not want to be in such dull company, that is all." He grinned broadly as the two gentlemen stopped dead, looking at each other uncertainly. "Why did you follow me here?"

Lord Davidson regained his composure a little bit, clearing his throat and coming a little closer. Oliver looked up at him from his chair, refusing to get up out of his seat nor even push himself up into a more formal sitting position. Instead, he continued to remain slumped in his chair, thinking Lord Davidson was an annoying sort of fellow and finding him more than a little irritating.

"I want to know if you are going to pursue Lady Amelia," Lord Davidson said, pulling a chair closer to Oliver and sitting down. "My coffers are not what they were, and my estate will not do well this year if I do not recover *some* of what I have lost."

Oliver rolled his eyes. "Even if I were to do so, why should I inform you?" he asked, slurring his words just a little. "I have no intention of helping you, Lord Davidson."

"You helped your friend last year," Lord Davidson said darkly, his expression growing rather grim as his companion wandered away, perhaps realizing the conversation was becoming a little more tense than he had anticipated. "Lord Marston made a good deal of money last year."

Oliver shifted a little uncomfortably in his chair. "I did not say anything in particular to Lord Marston," he said, his brandy sloshing from one side to the other in his glass as he moved. "He and I are very well acquainted, that is all. He knew some of the interests I had."

"And now I might know of one of these 'interests' also?" Lord Davidson queried, watching Oliver with a sharp eye as though he might blurt out the truth, should he look at him long enough. "I am desperate, Lord Montague. This would help me greatly."

Sighing, Oliver rested his head back against his chair

and regarded Lord Davidson. "I think, then, you ought to ensure you do not gamble any longer, Lord Davidson," he muttered, feeling a trifle more irritated. "Your coffers—or lack thereof—are none of my concern."

Lord Davidson's eyes narrowed, but Oliver turned his head away, wishing the gentleman would leave him alone so that he might drink his brandy in peace. The man's lack of skill in cards was nothing to do with him, and he had no intention of helping the fellow in any way.

"I must ask you, Lord Montague, if you are acquainted with Lady Thornhill?"

Oliver jerked visibly, reacting to the name at once. He narrowed his eyes and looked back towards Lord Davidson, who was watching him closely. "Do not question me, Davidson," he muttered, seeing the fellow begin to smile, although he forced himself not to react to the gentleman's expression. "It will not go well for you."

"I think I shall place a bet regardless, Lord Montague," Lord Davidson said, his voice holding a warning Oliver did not quite understand. "And I look forward to the time that I will be successful and gain the money I require."

Oliver waved his hand in Lord Davidson's direction, ignoring the fellow completely and letting out a long breath of relief when Lord Davidson finally got up and walked away. He had no intention of allowing Lord Davidson any insight into his considerations, especially since he would not be chasing after Lady Amelia, and regardless of what Lord Davidson might think, had no plans to express his previous acquaintance with Lady Thornhill, who was wife to the Marquess of Thornhill.

Lord Davidson could make any bet he wished, but Oliver would do nothing to attempt to fulfill it.

Sighing contentedly, Oliver lifted the glass of brandy to his lips and drained it, feeling the warmth spread through his chest and allowing his mind to cloud a little more. This was precisely what he needed. A quiet space where he might enjoy the finest French brandy and allow his thoughts to go wherever they pleased. Yes, this Season was going to be an excellent one, indeed.

CHAPTER SIX

"*I* do not think you want to be here at this moment, Lord Havisham."

Amelia looked up at Lord Havisham as he sat down beside her, his eyes fixed upon what she had been writing.

"I am quite contented to help you with your French," he told her quickly, a slightly strained expression on his face. "Although I am certain you have a greater grasp of the language than I!"

Amelia sighed heavily, then gestured to her paper. "I have been doing my very best to improve, but I find my pronunciation is less than perfect."

Lord Havisham rolled his eyes and sat back in his chair, looking at her with a wry smile. "And Lady Smithton thinks this will aid you in some way?"

Amelia nodded, although she could still not quite understand Lady Smithton's reasoning behind her insistence that she practice her French. "I have been practicing all week, and it is imperative that I have done so by this evening," she said, remembering what Lady Smithton had said. "Perhaps there is a particular gentleman she wishes me to meet."

"Mayhap that is the reason for it," Lord Havisham muttered, pushing himself forward in his chair with an effort. "I am to look over this and thereafter, assist you with any other difficulties you might have." He gave her a small, slightly rueful smile and picked up the paper. "I am not inclined towards languages, and yet my Eton education insisted I have a firm grasp of French. Lady Smithton knows this and, therefore, has forced me to use it." He chuckled wryly and then looked down at the paper. "I am sure that whatever Lady Smithton intends for this evening, you will find your French to come in very useful indeed."

Amelia smiled and waited until Lord Havisham went over the words she had written, leaning forward and nodding as he pointed out one or two small corrections. Thereafter, they enjoyed a long conversation in French, where he helped her here and there, leaving her feeling a good deal more confident with her grasp of the language.

"I think that will do for the present!" Lord Havisham exclaimed some twenty minutes later. "Unless there is anything else you wish to ask me?"

Seeing the desperately hopeful look in his eyes, Amelia let out a quiet laugh and shook her head. "I have nothing else to ask you, no," she said, laughing all the more when he let out a long sigh of relief. "I thank you for your help, however."

Lord Havisham smiled, slumping back in his chair in evident contentment. "You did not need much assistance," he said with a small shrug. "Which I am very grateful for, given I do not much like…" He laughed and waved a hand. "I do not need to repeat myself. Needless to say, I am glad you have done so well, and I shall be nearby this evening if you require my assistance again."

"I thank you," she answered, thinking to herself that the last ten days with Lady Smithton and what she now knew was called 'The Spinsters Guild' had been one of the most hope-filled times in her life thus far. "You have been very kind to me, Lord Havisham."

He smiled at her. "I am glad to be so," he answered. "And you have had a few interesting social occasions of late, I hope?"

"I have," Amelia answered, recalling how Lady Smithton, upon hearing she sang and enjoyed playing the pianoforte, had encouraged her to do so in front of Lord Burton's guests early the previous week. "I have been very nervous on occasion, but I have found the other young ladies, Lady Smithton, and yourself to be very encouraging."

Lord Havisham nodded, rose, and extended his hand. "Might I take you to the ballroom, Lady Amelia?" he asked, interrupting her thoughts. "We have to practice your waltz, I believe."

Amelia blinked, looking up at Lord Havisham and feeling her fear beginning to rise within her already. "No," she stammered, a little awkwardly, "I do not think that—"

"You can dance the waltz, Lady Amelia," came a

bright, confident voice as Lady Smithton walked into the room, smiling at her. "You have nothing to fear. Why do you look as though Lord Havisham has offered you something dreadful instead of something that will be greatly helpful to you?"

Amelia swallowed hard and shook her head. "I fear my leg will—"

"I will be most careful," Lord Havisham interrupted, gently. "There is nothing to fear."

"Lord Havisham is an *excellent* dancer," Lady Smithton said, not looking at Lord Havisham but continuing to smile encouragingly at Amelia. "He will be the most excellent of partners."

"I thank you, Lady Smithton."

Amelia hesitated, looking between Lord Havisham and Lady Smithton and seeing something pass between them, although nothing was said. There was a long look, with a small yet warm smile on Lord Havisham's face, which lit up his eyes and, in fact, his entire features, whilst Lady Smithton's cheeks colored just a little. Intrigued, Amelia remained silent, wondering if there was more to this friendship between Lady Smithton and Lord Havisham.

"Yes, dancing," Lady Smithton said briskly, giving herself a slight shake as she returned her attention to Amelia. "Come now; you must be brave. Lord Havisham will be an excellent partner and will do nothing to injure you."

"But not every partner will be so," Amelia stammered, feeling a little ungrateful. "If I am seen dancing, then might not other gentlemen seek me out?"

Lady Smithton smiled sympathetically. "They will, and that is what we wish them to do," she said pointedly. "But that does not mean you have to accept everyone who asks! You can easily refuse—and indeed, I would encourage you to do so to anyone who is either a little in their cups, appears clumsy or inconsiderate, or who is immediately rejected by either myself or Mrs. Peters. Besides which," she finished, laughing softly, "it will make you all the more intriguing if you only dance with some gentlemen and not others."

Amelia let out a long, slow breath and looked up at Lord Havisham, who had extended his hand again. She was not at all certain about dancing and was very afraid a gentleman might stand on her foot and wrench her painful leg in a manner that might force her to retire for the rest of the night. But then, she swallowed hard and reminded herself that, in order to make any progress within society, she had to be courageous. She had been so this last week, had she not? Lady Smithton had accompanied her to two separate soirees, a dinner, and had taken her in her carriage for a drive through Hyde Park during the fashionable hour. Mrs. Peters had accompanied her also, and Amelia had been glad to see just how delighted Mrs. Peters had been with all that was now occurring for Amelia. It had been astonishing to Amelia to realize just how much of a difference was made to her confidence when she had Lady Smithton by her side. The lady exuded strength and poise which, in turn, had encouraged Amelia. Her limp was just as pronounced, just as present, but with Lady Smithton giving it no attention whatsoever, Amelia found she herself did not give it as much consideration as before.

"Then we must practice the waltz," she murmured, accepting his hand and allowing him to help her to her feet. With Lady Smithton walking alongside them, the three walked from the room and slowly made their way to the ballroom.

"Lady Beatrice is to arrive soon," Lady Smithton stated as she surveyed Amelia's stance with a critical eye. "So you shall only have time to practice the waltz, which, I think, is more than enough for one session." She smiled at Amelia and gently straightened Amelia's hand as it rested on Lord Havisham's shoulder. "This is almost perfect, however, Lady Amelia. You are doing very well."

Amelia smiled back, trying to press down her anxiety as Lord Havisham held her both gently and with a firmness that encouraged her to trust him.

"I will support you, of course," he murmured, beginning to move carefully across the floor. "And you must inform me if you have any pain or difficulty, Lady Amelia."

Such was the strength of her concentration that Amelia said nothing in response. Her stomach was tight, her hands clammy, and her breathing ragged, feeling as though something would go wrong at any moment. It was not until some minutes had passed that she realized things were not going as badly as she might have thought. With Lord Havisham holding her tightly and moving carefully, Amelia found she was able to spin around the floor with more ease than she had expected. Breathing a little more easily, Amelia looked up at Lord Havisham and found herself smiling, actually finding a little more enjoyment from the dance than she had expected.

"I am terribly sorry to interrupt!"

Lord Havisham jerked, stumbled, and pulled Amelia forward as the sound of a gentleman's booming voice filled the ballroom. She let out a yelp of pain, with Lord Havisham only just managing to catch her and hold her steady before she tumbled to the floor.

"Oh, I do apologize," the gentleman said, coming a little closer to them with a broad smile on his face. "I thought to call upon you, Lady Amelia, and was informed you were at Lady Smithton's residence. I hope you do not mind, Lady Smithton?"

Amelia tried to catch her breath, bracing herself against the burning pain in her leg that fired up into her side. Lord Havisham had been doing very well, and she had been starting to let go of the tension that had otherwise filled her, only for it all to go very wrong indeed. Lord Havisham kept one hand about her waist and together, they walked slowly back towards Lady Smithton, who was glaring angrily at Lord Montague. Lord Montague did not appear to notice, however, looking directly back at Amelia with a broad smile settling on his face. His eyes strayed to Lord Havisham's hand at her waist and then the slowness with which they both walked, and something like understanding began to filter into his expression.

"Oh." Lord Montague cleared his throat, putting his hands behind his back and lowering his head, clearly aware now that he had caused a good deal more upset than he had had first been aware of. "Are you quite all right, Lady Amelia?"

She could not speak at first, such was her pain. She did not want to gasp with the agony of it, nor betray herself with a tight word or two. Lady Smithton must have realized she was struggling, for she stepped forward and gestured wildly towards Lord Montague.

"First of all, Lord Montague, you cannot march into my house and demand to see someone who is visiting here as my guest," Lady Smithton exclaimed as Lord Havisham leaned down to ask Amelia quietly whether she needed to sit down. "And secondly, I do not expect you to shout towards Lady Amelia, given you have just interrupted something of great importance."

Amelia, hating she had to show such weakness in front of Lord Montague, nodded towards Lord Havisham, who immediately led her away from Lady Smithton to ensconce her in a chair at the side of the room. Feeling the relief almost the moment she sat down, Amelia lifted her chin and looked back at Lord Montague, even though she knew quite certainly her face was a little red. *He* was the one at fault, she told herself. Therefore, she had nothing to be ashamed of.

"I do apologize, Lady Smithton." Lord Montague looked more than a little embarrassed, with his face downcast and his expression almost mournful. "It is only that I have not seen Lady Amelia for some time, and I did wonder if—"

"I have been at a few social occasions," Amelia interrupted before Lady Smithton could speak. "But perhaps they are not the sort of occasions that would interest you, Lord Montague." Much to her surprise, Amelia saw a dark expression flicker across Lord Montague's face, feeling immediately embarrassed that she had brought about such a change in his manner She had not meant anything by the remark, thinking back to how he had left Lord Burton's soiree rather quickly and had not seemed to enjoy it. "I—I merely meant—"

"I have been sorry not to see you at any of the social gatherings I have attended," he said briskly as though to throw aside her previous remark. "And I have not been able to forget your wonderful performance at Lord Burton's soiree last week. I must hope you will be able to do so again when you attend my small gathering which I am having on Tuesday next week." So saying, he plucked something from his pocket and, coming towards her, handed her the small, neat envelope with the red seal at the bottom. Looking up, she saw him hand one to Lady Smithton also, before looking at Lord Havisham with a slight awkwardness. "You—you are invited also, of course, Lord Havisham," he said, stammering a little. "I fear I have left your invitation at home."

Amelia could not help but smile, seeing Lord Montague had, in fact, not had any intention of inviting Lord Havisham but could not refuse to invite him now. Lord Montague caught her eye, seeing her understanding and her mirth at the situation and, much to her surprise, tilting his head to regard her a little more. Blushing with his regard, she saw a slow smile catch the corner of his lips, his eyes beginning to twinkle as he looked back at her.

She blushed all the more, embarrassed at her reaction to him and putting it down to the fact that Lord Montague was, of course, a fiendishly handsome gentleman. His shock of light brown hair swept over his brow, his square jaw, Roman nose, and broad shoulders giving her the impression of strength and fortitude. His eyes intrigued her, for they were a mixture of greens and blues and yellows, all swirling together and mixing with one another. The look shared between them reminded her swiftly of what she had witnessed passing between Lord Havisham and Lady Smithton, and such was her own embarrassment to be thinking of such a thing that she turned her head away, breaking their locked gaze.

"You are very kind, I am sure," Lord Havisham said, taking the attention away from Amelia's red cheeks. "I should be very glad to attend. Lady Smithton, you will permit me to take you in the carriage, I hope?"

Lady Smithton did not smile, her jaw set as she turned her sharp gaze onto Lord Havisham. Amelia winced inwardly, realizing Lady Smithton had not been as determined as Lord Havisham now was to accept the invitation.

"Capital!" Lord Montague boomed, his voice echoing around the room once more and making Amelia's skin prickle with the awareness of his presence. He could command a room, she was certain of it, for he indeed commanded all of her attention. Her heart began to soften towards Lord Montague, forgiving him quickly for his lack of thought as he had marched into Lady Smithton's ballroom and announced his intentions. He had not known she would be rehearsing the waltz with Lord

Havisham. And besides which, not only had he been kind enough to bring her an invitation to his planned soiree, but he had also complimented her, yet again, upon her musical performance. She recalled how he had come to her at Lord Burton's home and had spoken to her so kindly about how she had played and sang. Perhaps there was a goodness in him not everyone was permitted to see.

"I have Lady Beatrice arriving very soon," Lady Smithton said, having now finished glaring furiously at Lord Havisham. "I am afraid I shall have to ask you—"

"I have tarried on your kindness long enough," Lord Montague replied, bowing quickly towards Lady Smithton. "Particularly when I did not have an invitation to call upon either of you."

"Indeed," Lady Smithton murmured dryly, glancing towards Amelia as Lord Montague came a few steps closer to her. Amelia felt her heart quicken as he bent low, bending at the knees so that he might look up into her face.

"I am truly sorry for disturbing your dance and for causing you pain," he said, his expression a little troubled. "I did not intend to but, as Lady Smithton has pointed out, I ought not to have made such a noise when I first entered the house." He bowed his head low for a moment before lifting it. "I do hope you can forgive me."

"But of course," Amelia replied quickly, her heart slamming into her chest as he touched her fingers with his own. Lord Havisham had moved closer to Lady Smithton and was now talking in hushed tones, leaving Amelia and Lord Montague to speak without being overheard. "It was unintentional, I know."

He appeared relieved, although his smile was a little despondent. "You are very understanding, Lady Amelia. I do hope you will consider performing on the pianoforte, as you did at Lord Burton's? It would be the most marvelous part of the evening; I am quite certain of it."

She smiled but looked away, feeling anxious about doing so but knowing it would be only polite to agree. "I will consider it," she promised, making him beam at her as though she had given him the greatest of gifts. "Thank you again for your kind invitation."

Lord Montague nodded, thanked her, and removed his hand from hers, allowing Amelia to breathe properly again without feeling the tightness in her chest that his presence had brought. She watched him carefully as he made his farewells to Lord Havisham and then to Lady Smithton, apologizing once again before walking from the room. Amelia allowed herself a small smile, looking down at the invitation in her lap and thinking Lord Montague was, in fact, quite the gentleman. She had heard a whisper or two about him but had never once given him much consideration, given she knew him to be a man who sought out only the very best ladies for his company. And yet now, it seemed, he wanted to join him for his soiree, wanted her to be present as one of his guests! The very thought filled her with joy.

"Lady Amelia?"

She looked up at once, pulled away from her thoughts by the stern face of Lady Smithton and the angry-looking Lord Havisham."

"Yes?" she asked, fearing she had done something

wrong, although she could not imagine what it was. "Have I behaved inappropriately?"

"No, no, not at all!" Lady Smithton exclaimed, pressing down on Amelia's hand gently. "No, it is only that we feel must speak to you about Lord Montague." Her eyes were serious, although her expression was gentle. "He was very kind in bringing these invitations to us all, of course, and we are now to attend his gathering, given Lord Havisham has agreed to it." At this, she threw Lord Havisham an irritated glance, which Amelia finally understood meant she was annoyed with how he had gone about the matter. She had wanted the time to consider the invitation and the gentleman who had brought it, but instead, Lord Havisham had agreed without question.

"Lord Montague has something of a reputation," Lord Havisham said, sinking rather heavily into a chair next to Amelia. "He is not the sort of gentleman you should consider."

Amelia's heart began to sink from its heights of joy and happiness before beginning to make its way down to the depths of her spirits. Lord Montague had been very kind to her, had he not? He had done nothing but compliment her, speak well of her, and had been generous with his invitations to his soiree. What was it about him she ought to become aware of?

"He has a penchant for making improper advances to young ladies," Lady Smithton said quickly as though wanting to hurry the explanation. "I cannot think it wise for you to become too closely acquainted."

"I see," Amelia replied, looking from Lady Smithton

to Lord Havisham and then back down to the invitation in her lap. Her heart was sinking all the more now, given she had felt herself react strongly to his presence, aware he had managed to nudge at her interest. She had thought him handsome, had felt her heart quicken at his smile, and now was being told what she thought of him was not his true character. She had guessed him to be a popular gentleman, given his looks and, no doubt, his wealth, but she had never once considered him to be a rogue. It just proved to her she had not made a wise assessment of Lord Montague. Apparently, there was a good deal more to him than she had thought.

"He will want to converse with you, of course," Lady Smithton said, throwing a warning look towards Lord Havisham. "Someone will remain with you throughout the evening so that you are never alone with Lord Montague to engage in conversation."

"I am quite certain I can manage to converse with him," Amelia replied, a little confused. "I do not need any particular assistance in that matter."

"Of course," Lord Havisham interrupted, "but Lord Montague has a way of speaking that seems to encourage people to do what they have never once intended." Looking a little embarrassed at having to speak so openly, he shrugged one shoulder. "Young ladies who would never even dream of stepping away from their mother or their guardian to be alone with a gentleman have been found to do precisely that. Lord Montague can be very persuasive when he wants something, Lady Amelia."

Amelia shook her head, sighing inwardly. "I can hardly think he is interested in doing so with me," he said, seeing Lady Smithton's immediate frown. "I am sure there is another reason he has invited us to his soiree."

"And why should he not consider you, Lady Amelia?" Lady Smithton asked, her voice rising steadily. "You cannot think that just because you have a limp, Lord Montague would not choose to pursue you for sport?" She arched one eyebrow, and Amelia felt her mouth go dry, thinking of how Lord Montague had touched her hand as he had bent down to speak to her. He had been very attentive and seemingly very considerate, but mayhap, this was precisely because of what Lady Smithton was suggesting, although Amelia could not quite bring herself to believe it.

What was worse, however, was Amelia now felt a little blush creeping up her neck and into her face as a jolt of pleasure ran through her. Lord Montague had been very charming indeed, and she had reacted to him very strongly. Perhaps, she considered, feeling her stomach swirling with a mixture of nervousness and delight, she had been taken in by his charm, which it seemed he was well used to using to get what he desired. As much as she ought to feel horrified by his lack of gentlemanly intentions and as much as she ought to desire to remove herself entirely from his presence, Amelia found she felt a good deal of delight and appreciation that Lord Montague considered her either beautiful enough or charming enough for him to set his sights on. She had been introduced to other gentlemen this last week, of course, but not all of them had reacted to her as Lady Smithton had hoped, for some made it quite obvious that they noticed her limp, whilst others were rather dull and staid. Lord Montague was neither boring nor showed any particular interest in her limp, save to ask her if she had recovered from her stumble. He was the only gentleman who had made Amelia's heart quicken merely by allowing her eyes to rest on his, the only gentleman who had caught her interest thus far.

But you cannot allow yourself to do so any longer, she told herself sternly, as Lady Smithton's attention was caught by the arrival of Lady Beatrice. *You must do your best to separate yourself from Lord Montague, no matter what he seems to desire from you.*

Letting out a long breath, Amelia settled her shoulders and gave Lord Havisham a quick smile, seeing him sigh heavily as Lady Beatrice and Lady Smithton continued talking. Lord Havisham was to dance with Lady Beatrice now, in order to help her improve her steps, and Amelia had the distinct impression he did not particularly enjoy doing such a thing. And yet, he did them regardless, simply to help her as well as to aid Lady Smithton.

That, she told herself, watching as Lord Havisham rose to his feet, *is a gentleman who is truly committed and determined.* Although, whether it was that he was committed to 'The Spinsters Guild' or to Lady Smithton, Amelia could not quite make out.

"I think I must hope I will be able to find a gentleman with as much devotion as Lord Havisham," she commented quietly as Lord Havisham led Lady Beatrice to the floor, allowing Lady Smithton to resume her seat.

"Devotion?" Lady Smithton replied, glancing towards Amelia before turning her head back towards

Lord Havisham. "Yes, Lord Havisham is very involved with us, is he not?"

Amelia bit her lip, unsure whether or not she should press the matter but choosing, in the end, to do so. "He is, yes, and I have been very grateful for his help, but I do not think it is for our sake that he is so willing." She saw Lady Smithton's cheeks begin to color a gentle pink, seeing she did not turn back to look at Amelia. "In that regard, Lady Smithton, I think you are fortunate, indeed."

Nothing passed between them for a moment or two, and Amelia began to fear she had said more than she ought, only for Lady Smithton to sigh, smile and look back towards Amelia.

"Yes, I suppose I am very blessed in having Lord Havisham's willing presence here," Lady Smithton murmured, a small smile tugging at one corner of her lips. "And you are quite correct to state that he is devoted, Lady Amelia. It is something I have perhaps become used to, and so I am grateful to you for showing it to me once more."

A little relieved, Amelia said nothing more but smiled at Lady Smithton before returning her gaze to Lord Havisham and Lady Beatrice. She herself could not hope for a gentleman to care for her in the same way she suspected Lord Havisham cared for Lady Smithton, but at the very least, she might begin to hope she could secure a gentleman who would be devoted to her and to their marriage. A gentleman who would not turn away from her and chase after others, as she knew Lord Montague would do. She had to be prudent and yet hopeful at the same time, but any thought of Lord Montague could no longer be entertained. That, Amelia knew, was what was expected of her and what was wise—even if the thought of his smile sent her stomach tightening deliciously all over again.

CHAPTER SEVEN

"Thank you, Lord Montague, for your very kind invitation!"

Oliver sighed inwardly but forced a smile to his lips, not having any particular interest in the company of Lady Greenacre but knowing it had been a wise thought to invite her. Being the wife of the Marquess of Greenacre, it gave his little gathering some pomp, something that would be talked about by others in the days to come.

"I am very sorry your husband is unwell," he said, bowing over Lady Greenacre's hand. "Do you think he will recover soon?"

Lady Greenacre laughed merrily and waved a hand. "Of course he will," she replied, her eyes twinkling. "It is just his gout. You know very well that excess is the cause of such a malady and therefore, Lord Montague, I cannot help but think he has brought it on himself!"

Oliver nodded, murmured something about hoping Lord Greenacre would once more be able to join society, and then waved Lady Greenacre in. There were a few more guests still to greet.

"Lord...Davidson." His lips pressed together hard as Lord Davidson walked into the room, his eyes darting about the room whilst a cold smile flattened his lips. "You were not invited, I do not think."

Lord Davidson shrugged. "I thought to attend anyway," he replied as though this was something Oliver ought to have expected. "You know very well there are certain matters that are not yet at an end between us."

Oliver grimaced, feeling his tension rising but knowing full well it was his foolishness that was to blame. "I am not about to deliberately ruin my chances of success with the lady to ensure you lose yet more coffers," he stated, quite firmly, as Lord Davidson's eyes narrowed. "That is what you believe, is it not?"

Lord Davidson shrugged. "I do not know quite what to think," he stated, with a lift of one shoulder. "After all, you stated very clearly you would not partake in any bets made in Whites, and now, it seems, you have agreed to do so regardless of your previous concerns."

"That is because I have very little choice, as well you know," Oliver replied angrily as one hand curled into a fist, his ire burning hot with a deep and unrelenting fury. "But I, for one, shall behave honorably and whilst I will pursue the lady in question, if she rejects me—as I hope she will—then you will have nothing from the bet you have placed." Forcing himself not to react any further, he shook out his hand, trying to bring down his anger to a quiet coolness so that none of the other guests, who were watching, would see his fury. "I intend to behave honorably, as much as I can."

Lord Davidson snorted. "No, Lord Montague, that is not what you are to do." Stepping a little closer, he looked Oliver straight in the eye. "You are to succeed. I need that money. Therefore, if you do not succeed, then I shall have to do as I have threatened. You know such a thing will not go very well for either you or the lady."

"I am well able to steal a kiss without too much difficulty," Oliver retorted, only for Lord Davidson to hold up one hand, angering Oliver further.

"You did not read the bet carefully enough, I believe," he murmured, making a cold shiver run through Oliver's frame. "You must not just steal a kiss, Lord Montague. You must have her confess her love for you."

Oliver stared into Lord Davidson's face, his heart stopping completely for a moment. It was one thing to have a young lady swept away by his charms to the point that she would let him take a kiss or two, but quite another to encourage a lady's true affections. Yes, he was quite certain some of the young ladies he had tempted in the past had allowed a fondness for him into their heart, but he would never once have thought any of them had fallen in love with him.

"I needed as many gentlemen to bet against me as possible," Lord Davidson explained, softly. "To steal a kiss is much too easy for you. Therefore, you must have the lady profess her love for you in order for me to win the wager." He chuckled, shaking his head at Oliver's foolishness. "There are many who think you cannot charm a lady into admitting such a thing, for that would take a degree of dedication on your part, and you are much more inclined towards a quick seduction."

Oliver blinked rapidly, his heart beginning to race with the enormity of what was now facing him.

"That is the bet, Lord Montague," Lord Davidson finished, stepping back from Oliver and grinning in evident contentment, clearly aware that Oliver was a little shaken by this news. "You cannot escape it now."

And without another word, Lord Davidson stepped away from Oliver, wandering into the room in an amicable fashion as though he had every right to be a part of the present company. It was all Oliver could do not to pursue him, grasp him by the arm, and propel him from the room, even though he knew that to do so would make matters all the worse.

An icy hand grasped his heart and sent rivulets of cold all through him, making Oliver shudder for a moment. He could still recall what it had been like to receive Lord Davidson's note, expressing what he had done and expecting Oliver to do precisely as he had been directed without hesitation. Quite how Lord Davidson had discovered Oliver had enjoyed a particularly warm acquaintance with the Lady Thornhill last Season, Oliver was not quite certain, but evidently, the fellow had done so and now fully intended to share such information with the Marquess of Thornhill, should Oliver refuse to agree to do as Lord Davidson asked.

Regardless, he had considered the matter, and thus, had taken himself to Whites to look at the betting book. He had not looked long at it but had glanced at the words and the gentleman's signature, leaving Oliver with no doubt that the fellow intended to do just as he had threatened, should Oliver refuse to agree. Lady Thornhill had been a very lovely acquaintance, and he had enjoyed a few short weeks of her company, but it had come to a swift end, and Oliver had thought himself glad to be parted from her in the end. The Marquess was known to be a cruel sort of gentleman, although a good deal older than his wife, which was why she had sought out perhaps more gentle company. However, Oliver knew all too well the Marquess would do all he could to punish Oliver for what he had done, should he ever come to hear of it. The Marquess was both powerful and wealthy. There was a great deal he could do, should he decide to do so, making Oliver consider him a formidable enemy. It had been unwise, he knew, to have given in to his desires for Lady Thornhill, but she had been so very willing, and he had always liked beautiful things. He had cared nothing for her sorrows and her struggles in her marriage to Lord Thornhill, but had used her for his enjoyments. When she had begun to cling to him, when she had begun to speak to him and cry on his shoulder over her unhappiness, he had not had any other choice but to bring things to a close, knowing full well she would not speak of it to anyone and neither would he do so. Now, however, it seemed someone had taken notice of their closeness and had perhaps come to the simple conclusion. Lord Davidson was now using that conclusion against Oliver, forcing him to do what he did not want to do.

Oliver had thought about simply offering Lord Davidson money instead of having to go through with the bet, but then he had shied away from the idea. Lord

Davidson might then try to take *more* money from Oliver, perhaps using the very same threat, and Oliver would have no choice but to give it to him. With the betting book, it seemed Lord Davidson's only intention was to gain some money back and to prove to his friends he was not as unlucky as they believed him to be. Either that or perhaps he had not realized he could use the same threat again.

Cursing himself that he had not taken the time to read all that had been written in the betting book, Oliver shook his head, closed his eyes, and let his breath rattle out from him. Lord Davidson was not asking merely for Oliver to behave as he had done before, in pursuing young ladies in order to be the first to kiss their innocent lips, but rather to go a step further and encourage Lady Amelia's affections to the point she would state herself in love with him. Oliver did not want to do so, of course, for Lady Amelia was not at all the sort of young lady he would normally seek out, given she had a limp and was, he had presumed, quite unable to dance or the like, and besides which, there was something nudging his conscience when it came to that particular lady. To make her fall in love with him might be a great and somewhat difficult task, but whilst Oliver believed he could do so, he found himself entirely unwilling. Lady Amelia already had enough difficulties when it came to the ton, and thus, he did not want to add to her burden. To have her fall in love with him, only to reveal he cared nothing for her and had done so only to win a bet, might very well break her entirely.

But what choice did he have?

"Lord Montague?"

A quiet, slightly uncertain voice reached his ears, forcing him away from his thoughts and returning him to the present. He turned, an expectant smile on his face, only for it to die away at the sight of Lady Amelia standing before him, with her companion a little behind her.

She was utterly resplendent. With a gown of light green that lit up her eyes, and dark tresses held back, seed pearls and a ribbon or two flowing through the waves of her hair, Oliver found himself lost for words.

She took a step forward, her limp pronounced, but Oliver barely even noticed it. Reaching out, he took her hand and bowed over it, pressing his lips to the back of her hand very quickly but hearing her swift intake of breath.

"Thank you for attending this evening," he said, truly appreciative that she had come. "You look quite wonderful, Lady Amelia." Lifting his head, he smiled at her and looked into her eyes, expecting her to blush, to turn her head and look away, smiling quietly at his compliment.

Instead, she looked back at him silently for a moment or two, no smile on her face and no lightness in her eyes. It was as though she were judging him, considering him, and trying to work through the compliments he had given her as though they meant more.

"Good evening, Lord Montague."

Mrs. Peters pressed forward, forcing Oliver to let go of Lady Amelia's hand and seeing her turn to walk away from him without another word. A little perplexed, he tried to smile at Mrs. Peters, stumbling over his words as he welcomed her. Mrs. Peters nodded, her expression tight as she hurried after her charge.

How very odd.

Oliver's frown grew steadily as he watched Lady Amelia, seeing how she made her way towards Lord Havisham and Lady Smithton, who had arrived some ten minutes earlier. They greeted her warmly, and she smiled and nodded at them in a way she had not done towards him. A little injured—although unable to explain why he felt such frustration when he had been treated so by many young ladies wary of him—Oliver continue to watch Lady Amelia with a steady gaze, wondering what it was he had done that had caused her to treat him so.

Unfortunately for Oliver, the entire evening seemed to pass in a very similar fashion. Whenever he sought Lady Amelia out, either Mrs. Peters, Lord Havisham, or Lady Smithton would be present with her. She said very little to him on each occasion, showing no particular interest in continuing their conversation and clearly unwilling to harness the opportunity to further their acquaintance, such as it was.

"I think I have to declare defeat already," he murmured, picking up a glass from the tray and seeing Lord Davidson standing nearby. "The lady will not so much as share more than a few words with me!"

Lord Davidson rolled his eyes. "You know you must succeed," he stated, bluntly. "That is my expectation, Lord Montague. Else there will be consequences." He chuckled darkly, making a shudder run down Oliver's spine. "Besides, out of all the young ladies in society, Lady Amelia is surely the easiest young lady to capture, Lord Montague! She is not going to be considered by anyone else, so I am quite certain she will be flattered by your attention, given she will be so unused to receiving even a momentary glance from a gentleman." He grinned at Oliver, who turned away from the man, feeling a little sickened. That was quite true, of course, but he did not want to hear it so callously spoken by Lord Davidson, who had, it seemed, a good deal more cruelty within him than Oliver had expected.

"I do not notice her limp," Oliver retorted, with a sharpness to his tone he had not intended. "I do not think that makes Lady Amelia any less of a lady than those who surround her."

Lord Davidson stared at him for a moment, then let out a chuckle that made Oliver wince inwardly at what he had just revealed.

"Goodness, this may be more difficult for you than I had first considered!" he laughed, making Oliver turn away entirely. "She has quite caught your attention, Lord Montague, has she not? And you have never once felt such a thing before, I am quite certain."

Angry with Lord Davidson's behavior and even more upset with his own foolishness, Oliver muttered darkly under his breath. He began to weave his way through the guests, knowing he ought soon to be beginning the musical part of the evening but feeling the need to find a little solace for a short time.

Walking from the drawing-room, he slipped into the ballroom, his steps hurried for he knew he could not be away from his guests for long. The door to the gardens was open, and he stepped through it at once, taking a long breath of the cooler night air and trying to use it to calm his anger. He disliked Lord Davidson intensely and to have spoken so openly to him had been more than foolish. Now Lord Davidson would continue to mock, to press, and to otherwise anger him in ways Oliver had never thought possible.

His head slammed into his hands as he sank onto a nearby bench, his heart quailing for a moment as he considered Lady Amelia and what he was now expected to do. There was something about Lady Amelia that *did*, in fact, capture his heart. He wanted to think of her as he did every other young lady of his acquaintance, but whenever he did so, there was something within him that rebelled at the idea. He wanted to reject such a thought, wanted to turn away from it given it felt both strange and delightful in equal measure, but regardless of what he wished, it remained within him. By all accounts, he ought to have given Lady Amelia nothing more than a quick glance, given she had such a frailty with her leg, but for some reason, he had not been able to do so. She was beautiful, yes, but there was something more about her that tugged at his heart. He wanted to go to her, wanted to converse with her and discover more about her. He had *never* wanted to do such a thing before and, if he were being truthful with himself, Oliver would admit he was a little frightened by such a desire. Young ladies were nothing but sport to him, were nothing but easy entertainment that brought him both satisfaction and a pride he had so often let fill his chest and his heart. Now, however, he felt ashamed at the thought of pursuing Lady Amelia in the same way as he had done to so many others. Was it just because he did not want to bring her more shame when he knew the ton looked down at her, laughed at her, and mocked her for being less than perfect? Or was there more to his considerations than that?

The sound of a quiet conversation caught his ears, and before he could stand up, two figures appeared out of the growing darkness, coming towards him. One, he recognized, was Lady Amelia, who was walking with her arm in Lady Smithton's, who was supporting her. They were talking quietly together, with Lady Smithton saying something that was making Lady Amelia nod fervently.

"Ladies," he began, getting to his feet and smiling at them both, inclining his head and hoping they were not startled by his presence. "You have done the same as I, it seems, and have come to the gardens for a little air."

Lady Smithton smiled, but it did not reach her eyes. "As you see," she agreed, spreading out her hand. "But we are returned now, given the air is growing a little chilled."

"Then might I escort you back inside?" he asked, coming a little closer and offering his arm to them both, although he presumed Lady Smithton would refuse him, given the way she was currently regarding him. "I should not like anyone to stumble, given I have been the cause of your previous one, Lady Amelia."

Lady Amelia looked a little surprised at his remark before giving him a small smile, darting a glance towards Lady Smithton as she did so.

At that moment, Oliver understood precisely what

had occurred. Lady Smithton, in being Lady Amelia's particular friend, had taken great pains to explain to her precisely the sort of gentleman Oliver was. Therefore, Lady Amelia had decided she would not react warmly to his company nor his conversation, which was, he had to admit, very wise indeed—although it certainly made his task a good deal more complicated.

"Lady Amelia, why do you not take Lord Montague's arm?" Lady Smithton suggested, albeit with a good deal of reluctance. "It is not far, and I shall walk alongside you, of course."

Lady Amelia hesitated for a moment before lifting her hand from Lady Smithton's arm and then moving forward to place it in his. He smiled down at her, her features lit by the light from the doorway and felt his heart quicken as she gave him a brief smile in response.

"Shall we?" he asked, walking forward and gesturing for Lady Smithton to lead the way. They said nothing as they walked, and with only a short distance between the open door and the drawing-room, Oliver found it difficult to come up with something to say that Lady Amelia might respond to.

His mind struggled to remove itself from the quagmire that seemed to hold it in place. His thoughts were slow and sluggish, giving him none of the answers he desired and certainly becoming more of a struggle the longer he contemplated things. This was not at all what he had expected, for he had always found it very easy indeed to talk to young ladies without any difficulty whatsoever.

"Do you still wish me to play this evening, Lord Montague?"

Thankfully, Lady Amelia spoke before he had even thought of a single question to ask her. Relieved, he looked down at her and saw her expression a little uncertain, although he did not know whether it was from walking with him or from anxiety over playing the pianoforte in front of his guests.

"I would very much like you to play, yes," he told her, choosing his words with great care. "But that does not mean you must accept, Lady Amelia. I would not force you to do so, only to state that I would be honored if you would bless my house with your wonderful talent. Your playing and singing have such beauty that they quite take my breath away."

Lady Amelia blushed furiously and dropped her head, making Oliver smile. He doubted she had been given many compliments before and it was quite clear she was unused to reacting to them. Most other young ladies would cling onto a compliment, fawn over it and bat their eyes at him in response, whereas Lady Amelia said nothing and continued to look away. Oliver found himself liking her all the more for it, for she was clearly humble and very gracious indeed, although he did want her to be fully aware of just how well he thought of her playing. "I will not press you, of course. I just wish others might share in the enjoyment I know will come from your performance."

"Then I feel as though I cannot refuse," she answered, glancing up at him a little doubtfully as if she did not quite trust his words. "I will play two songs if that will suffice?"

His heart leaped in his chest just as a broad smile spread across his face, both astonishing him with their swiftness. "That would be wonderful indeed," he answered, blinking in surprise at his joyous reaction. "Thank you, Lady Amelia."

She smiled at him then and, for the first time that evening, Oliver felt as though she were smiling at him without restraint nor hindrance. There appeared to be no sense of holding back from him, for her smile reached her eyes and made her entire face light up.

He held onto that smile for a moment, feeling his heart lift and a sense of satisfaction wash over him. They had managed to make a connection at least, however small, and for that, he was grateful. What he was meant to do thereafter, in attempting to bring her closer to him when it was clear Mrs. Peters and Lady Smithton would be doing all they could to prevent him from doing so, he was not certain.

However, for the moment, Oliver decided he would be glad for her company and her willingness to sing and play for his guests. The rest of his questions and concerns could be considered later.

CHAPTER EIGHT

"*I* would like to call upon you if I may."

Those words rang around Amelia's head as she sat in the window seat of her uncle's library, looking out at nothing in particular and letting her mind fill with thoughts of Lord Montague. Last evening had gone well, despite her determination to stay far away from Lord Montague. Somehow, he had managed to seek her out as she had taken a short walk with Lady Smithton and thereafter had offered to escort them both back to the drawing-room. Lady Smithton had not accepted, of course, for she would not want any rumors to come from the sight of her walking, arm in arm, with Lord Montague, but for Amelia, there had been no such concerns given Lady Smithton was chaperoning her. She had taken his arm hesitantly, feeling all manner of emotions and wishing she felt nothing of the sort, for he brought about such confusing feelings within her that Amelia did not quite know what to do. She had not mentioned a single word of her feelings to either Lady

Smithton or Mrs. Peters, who had become very close friends in a short space of time and who would, of course, share any such insights with each other should Amelia reveal them.

Last evening, she had also had the opportunity to speak to two other gentlemen Lady Smithton had introduced her to on a previous occasion. One was Lord Robertson, who hailed from Scotland but had come to London to seek a bride, whilst the other was a quieter, yet handsome gentleman, Lord Villeroy. He was clearly a well-educated gentleman, and she had been given the opportunity to converse with him in French, which had seemed to both delight and impress him. Lady Smithton had encouraged the connection, which Amelia had been glad for, but had to admit there was no sense of connection with Lord Villeroy. He was handsome, yes, and clearly intelligent, but he very rarely asked her any questions, preferring instead to talk about his interests. Nor had he asked her to dance, asked to call on her, or even stated he hoped they might meet again very soon. Perhaps he was simply another charming gentleman who did not want to have a wife with so obvious a flaw.

"Amelia?"

She jerked in surprise, her leg twinging with pain as she swung her legs around from the window seat, so they dangled over the edge, only a few inches from the floor. "Yes?" she called, not quite certain who was seeking her but knowing the library door was open. "Uncle?"

It was indeed her uncle who came to the door, only for another gentleman to step through after him. Amelia's cheeks flared at once as she pushed herself forward, her feet firmly on the floor as she ignored the spiraling pain that shot up her leg as she did so.

"Uncle," she murmured, inclining her head and lowering her gaze, aware of just how quickly her heart was beating and silently wondering where Mrs. Peters was at this moment. "Good afternoon."

"Here you are, Amelia," her uncle said, loud enough for the words to bounce around the room. "You have a visitor."

Amelia swallowed hard and curtsied quickly in the direction of Lord Montague, gritting her teeth against the pain that came from her action. She was well used to it by now, for it hit her every time she curtsied, but from the sharp look in Lord Montague's eye, she wondered if he was aware of her struggle.

"And he has asked my permission to court you," her uncle continued, making Amelia's eyes flare with surprise, only for her to duck her head in embarrassment at his lack of propriety. Now was not the moment to speak of such things, not when Lord Montague was present, but it seemed the Earl cared very little for when and where certain remarks should be made, given he continued regardless.

"I have, of course, agreed," he continued, waving a hand. "I was quite certain you would not have any objections, Amelia, given you have had no other callers either this Season or last!" He chuckled and looked towards Lord Montague as though this was a very humorous remark, although Lord Montague did not so much as smile, Amelia saw. Perhaps he was not as cruel as Lady Smithton believed him.

Be careful.

The warning in her head began to ring furiously as Lord Montague bowed again, smiling at her warmly. He was so very handsome and very charming indeed, but she knew all too well of his reputation. Lady Smithton and Lord Havisham would not have collaborated to make up such a story, which meant there could only be truth within it.

"I do hope you do not think badly of me for being so eager in my pursuit," Lord Montague said as her uncle looked on, approvingly. "Ever since you played the pianoforte at Lord Burton's townhouse I have been quite unable to remove you from my mind. The only way to resolve the struggle I have at present is to seek to court you so that my fears that another gentleman may do so before me are completely allayed."

The Earl laughed aloud at this remark, however, making Amelia flush crimson with embarrassment.

"I do not think you need concern yourself in that regard, Lord Montague," he said as though Amelia herself were not present. "My niece is not being actively pursued by any gentleman. I believe you are the first to take notice of her!"

Amelia closed her eyes and lowered her head, feeling tears sting in the corners of her eyes. Her uncle could be so very callous in what he said, even though she did not believe he intended to be so. He just did not think about the consequences such a manner of speaking could have on Amelia's spirit.

"Then I will consider myself fortunate indeed," she heard Lord Montague say, keeping her head low as heat burned in her cheeks. "And I must add that I think the other gentlemen very foolish indeed to ignore such a splendid lady as Lady Amelia. *They* are the fools, Lord Stockbridge. How glad I am that my own heart has been captured by Lady Amelia!"

She blinked rapidly, forcing her tears away and looking directly at Lord Montague as she lifted her head. His lips were pulled in a thin line, tight with anger, whilst his eyes shone with sympathy and understanding. Her heart began to ache, seeing him in a new light and feeling as though he might, in fact, be able to behave differently towards her as he had done with all the other young ladies of his acquaintance.

"Very good, very good," Lord Stockbridge muttered, clearly a little thrown by Lord Montague's swift retort. Looking all about him, he gave Lord Montage a smile. "I have a small matter of business to attend to, I am afraid."

"But of course," Lord Montague replied hurriedly. "I would not prevent you from returning to it, Lord Stockbridge, particularly when I did not inform you of my visit in advance."

Lord Stockbridge smiled, then gestured to Amelia. "Pray, sit with Lady Amelia for a time, if you wish. I shall ensure her companion is brought to her, so you have no need to fear for any impropriety." He winked broadly at Lord Montague, making Amelia cringe. "She will not force you into anything you do not yet wish to commit to, given she can barely rise from her chair without assistance!" Laughing, he slapped Lord Montague on the shoulder and then hurried from the room, leaving Amelia flushed red with mortification all over again.

"I am sorry, Lady Amelia."

Being left alone with Lord Montague, having been spoken of in such an embarrassing manner by her uncle, and now hearing Lord Montague apologize as though he had been the cause of her uncle's behavior left Amelia feeling entirely uncertain. She swayed for a moment, glancing at the chairs to her left and then to the open door on her right, not sure whether she should ask Lord Montague to sit down or if she should insist he retreat to the passageway until Mrs. Peters joined them.

"Might I help you to a chair?"

He had made the decision for her, it seemed, moving forward to offer his arm and smiling at her kindly. Amelia had no choice but to accept, aware of just how heavily she leaned on him as she walked.

"Might I ask what occurred to pain your leg so badly?" he asked as she sat down. "I do not mean to be rude, and if you do not wish to share it with me, then I apologize for asking such an impertinent question."

Given she was still embarrassed from her uncle's behavior, Amelia sighed inwardly and decided she may as well speak openly to Lord Montague. "I fell from a tree when I was a child," she said, not quite able to meet his firm gaze. "It was my own doing, of course."

"That must have been very painful indeed," he replied gently, his expression soft as she finally looked into his eyes. "I am sorry. Does it pain you often?"

She nodded, looking at him and feeling a small weight roll from her shoulders. "It does. But I am able to walk and sometimes able to dance. I must rest thereafter, that is all."

He smiled at her, a slight embarrassment in his gaze. "Perhaps we might dance together one evening," he suggested, his voice filled with a hopefulness that did not quite reach his eyes. Was it because he expected her to agree to it almost at once, believing she could think of nothing better than to be in his arms?

Amelia frowned, lifting one shoulder in a small shrug. "I could not say, Lord Montague," she began, only just then, recalling what her uncle had said regarding Lord Montague's intentions for her. He had come to court her, her uncle had said, had come to ask his permission which, of course, Lord Stockbridge had granted at once. She blinked rapidly, astonishment filling her all over again as she studied him. What was his intention in doing such a thing? Surely it could not be anything true? Lady Smithton had warned her Lord Montague was not to be trusted. Therefore, she would have to take Lady Smithton at her word.

"You do not care for me, I think, Lady Amelia."

His honesty surprised her, leaving her struggling to respond honestly.

"I should have spoken to you before I spoke to your uncle, I suppose," he continued, looking at her with a somewhat apologetic gaze. "But I feared you would refuse me. I can tell Lady Smithton does not wish for you to engage with me."

"Perhaps she is wise enough to know it might be only a fleeting encounter," Amelia challenged, finally finding enough courage within her to speak as openly and as honestly as he had done. "You cannot imagine I am unaware of your reputation, Lord Montague." She swallowed quickly, her throat a little dry as she forced herself to speak without hesitation, stating things as clearly as she could. "I know very well what it is you incline yourself towards, Lord Montague."

Much to her surprise, he flushed and dropped his gaze. "I could not imagine you did not know of it," he answered, his voice low. "And I can well understand Lady Smithton would urge you to stay far from me, Lady Amelia. And yet, I must hope within that, there is a slight hesitation in your mind over me."

A little flushed herself, given her honesty in her speech, Amelia paused before she answered, knowing what Lord Montague was hoping for but finding she was not quite able to give him what he desired. "I trust Lady Smithton's judgment," she answered slowly. "And I do intend to follow it."

"So you will not accept my courtship," he stated, sounding more than a little disappointed. "You will not even give me the opportunity to prove myself?"

Amelia was about to open her mouth and state that no, she could not give him the chance to prove himself, only to find there was something sticking in her throat, something preventing her from doing just what she intended. She knew she ought to insist there could be no courtship, no furthering of their acquaintance, but the look in his eyes and the expectant hope in his expression prevented her from doing so.

"I would have preferred you had asked me at the first, Lord Montague," she said, thinking about what she had to do. "In speaking to my uncle, I will now find it very difficult indeed to refuse you."

"Then allow me to court you for a short time," he said eagerly, sitting forward in his chair as though to convince her by his earnestness. "If we do not suit or if I prove myself to be the rogue you believe me to be—a reputation I know I have earned—then I will tell your uncle I have decided it cannot be." He smiled and shrugged. "I will take the blame for it all. I will tell him of my reputation, if he is not aware of it already, and will state I don't think we will suit. Will that allay some of your fears?"

Amelia bit her lip, knowing there was a good deal more to what Lord Montague was proposing than he realized. Given she was affected by his presence, she could not be certain that being courted by him would not give rise to further feelings, which she would then have to continue to battle in order to remove him from her heart and mind completely. Besides which, it was not what Lady Smithton would advise, and Amelia knew very well Lady Smithton's considerations were worth a very great deal.

"It seems I have no choice but to accept," she said slowly, hating that her heart turned over at her decision, that her spirits lifted higher than before. "But I will be on my guard against you, Lord Montague," she finished, trying to bring as much determination to her own heart as to her voice. "I must believe you are just as much the rogue as ever, and your intentions towards me may not be as they seem."

Lord Montague looked distinctly uncomfortable at this remark and dropped his gaze, running one hand through his fair hair before nodding, clearing his throat as he did so.

"Very well," he murmured, just as a maid walked into the room bearing a tray which held a teapot, cups and saucers, and a few small delicacies. "I thank you, Lady Amelia, and hope I might prove myself to you in the days and weeks to follow."

"I hope so also," Amelia found herself replying without having had any intention of saying anything of the sort. Realizing she had betrayed herself, she tried to focus on the maid and the tea tray, praying he would not notice her reddening cheeks. "Might you send for Mrs. Peters also, please?"

The maid nodded, bobbed a quick curtsy, and scurried from the room, leaving Amelia with the distinct impression that her uncle had not managed to inform Mrs. Peters of Lord Montague's arrival—possibly deliberately so. Praying it would not be long before Mrs. Peters joined them, Amelia began to pour the tea, keeping her eyes off Lord Montague and focusing entirely on the task at hand.

"Goodness gracious, what is the meaning of this?"

Amelia looked up at once, the color draining from her cheeks as she saw the horrified expression on Mrs. Peters face as she hurried into the library.

"Mrs. Peters, thank you for joining us," she began, as Mrs. Peters eyes, still wide, turned towards her. "My uncle said he would send for you, but perhaps he forgot to do so, given he was busy with some very pressing matters." Amelia looked pointedly at Mrs. Peters, hoping she would understand, and thankfully saw Mrs. Peters give the tiniest of nods. "There is more I must tell you, but for the present, might you join us for tea? I would be glad for your company, Mrs. Peters."

"As would I," Lord Montague said, earning himself a somewhat dark look from Mrs. Peters. "I am certain we will be much better acquainted very soon, Mrs. Peters."

Amelia gave her companion a small, apologetic smile, and thankfully, Mrs. Peters chose to sit down without further comment. Amelia knew there would be a good deal to discuss once Lord Montague had left and, from the way Mrs. Peters had reacted to Lord Montague's presence, Amelia felt uncertain as to how Lady Smithton would respond to her very sudden and unexpected news. Part of her began to dread speaking to Lady Smithton again, to explain to her what had occurred. Would she be angry with her for going against her wise counsel? Reprimand her for wasting her time when it was clear she had suitors willing to look at her, regardless of her limp? Or would she understand Amelia had been in a difficult situation, what with Lord Montague going to her uncle first? Swallowing hard and feeling nothing but doubt and uncertainty, Amelia handed the cup of tea to Lord Montague and gestured for him to help himself to the cakes set out before him. She now longed for this visit to be over so that she might speak candidly to Mrs. Peters, in preparation for what she would have to then say to Lady Smithton.

"I came to you just as soon as I could."

Amelia pressed her lips together tightly to force

herself not to say another word. Lady Smithton was staring at her as though she had never seen Amelia before in her life, her face a little pale and her eyes lacking their usual sparkle. Having told Lady Smithton that Lord Montague was now to court her, it seemed the astonishment of Amelia's news had overwhelmed her.

"I have spoken to the Earl," Mrs. Peters added, her voice and expression grave, "but he insists Amelia accept Lord Montague's courtship. I did express my concern, given Lord Montague has such a dire reputation, but I'm afraid the Earl merely brushed aside my concerns and told me it was quite clear Lord Montague intended to court Lady Amelia."

Amelia swallowed hard, wanting to state, for the second time, that it had not been her intention to accept Lord Montague, but her uncle would not have permitted her to refuse. She would not have said, however, there was a part of her that was glad for such an arrangement, a part of her that hoped Lord Montague was not about to turn around and treat her as he had done so many others. After all, said a small voice, he had not courted any of the other young ladies he had sought out, had he?

"I—I must say, this is quite unexpected," Lady Smithton murmured, sounding quite breathless. "Lord Montague is not at all the sort of gentleman to do such a thing and yet..." She frowned, looking steadily at Amelia. "Yet, he has decided to court you?"

"It is a surprise, to be sure," Amelia admitted, feeling a little stung by Lady Smithton's evident astonishment. "I cannot pretend part of me does not hope there may be a genuine interest on his part, whereas I know the truth must be that there is another motivation he is hiding." She held her breath, wondering if Lady Smithton would contradict her, would tell her she was mistaken, but to her disappointment, Lady Smithton began to nod, slowly.

"There must be," she admitted, looking at Amelia with concern. "Lord Montague is, from what I understand, a wealthy gentleman with very little financial concerns. However, he would not be the first gentleman to hide the truth from society. You must be very careful, Lady Amelia."

Amelia managed a small smile. "Then you do not blame me for accepting him?"

Lady Smithton looked horrified. "No, of course, I do not!" she exclaimed, one hand pressed against her heart. "I can understand your difficulties entirely. I was also in a similar circumstance, given I had no choice whatsoever when it came to my husband." She shook her head sadly, a far-off look in her eyes. "It is our fate, it seems, to be told what we must do and what we must not. I count myself very fortunate indeed to have been allowed such freedom as I now experience."

It was on the tip of Amelia's tongue to ask whether or not Lady Smithton would be willing to give up such freedom in order to marry again—having Lord Havisham in mind—but a quick glance towards Mrs. Peters told her she ought not to say anything.

"Therefore," Lady Smithton said, giving herself a small shake, "here is what we shall do. You shall continue your courtship with Lord Montague, Lady Amelia, given you have no choice but to do so. Mrs. Peters or I shall always accompany you, and we shall all continue to seek out a reason for his eagerness to court you. Lord Havisham will be more than able to assist with this particular matter, given he can frequent places I cannot." She gave Amelia a small smile, which, whilst encouraging Amelia a little, did not prevent her from feeling a small sense of guilt that she had not told Lady Smithton everything—namely that she found herself secretly a little glad to be courting Lord Montague. "Have no fear, Lady Amelia," Lady Smithton finished, sounding a little more resolute. "You shall not be left alone in this circumstance. Together, we shall do our very best to protect you and remove you from this unfortunate situation—and to place you back amongst gentlemen who are a good deal more suited to you than Lord Montague."

"I thank you," Amelia replied gratefully. "As always, you are very kind, Lady Smithton."

"There is no need to thank me," Lady Smithton replied, getting up to ring the bell for tea. "I am glad to help, Lady Amelia. Truly."

CHAPTER NINE

*T*he day was very fine indeed, with the sun shining beautifully in a cloudless, blue sky, the flowers resplendent in all their glory and a delicate butterfly or two making their way from flower to flower.

And yet, Oliver felt nothing but dismay.

"It is a beautiful day, is it not?"

He cleared his throat, looking down at Lady Amelia as she walked beside him, her face upturned to the sky without any clear desire to hide her skin from the sun, as so many other young ladies might do. "Yes," he murmured, aware of how she leaned on him as they walked. "It is a very fine day, and I am glad to share it with you, Lady Amelia." This, he had to admit to himself, was truthful indeed, for there was something about Lady Amelia's company that brought joy to his heart. They had been courting for a little over a sennight now, and he had called upon her almost every day, wanting to ensure he did all he could to impress his feelings upon her. Feelings he was having to convince himself he did not truly feel.

"Oh, good afternoon, Lord Montague!"

"Good afternoon, Lord Chadderfield," he replied, aware the newly titled Viscount Chadderfield—who had held the title for a little over a year now—was both arrogant and more of a gossip than any lady he had ever encountered. "And might I inquire as to whom it is you are walking with this fine day?" He smiled politely at the young lady standing beside Lord Chadderfield, taking in her delicate frame, sweet smile, and the sharpness of her eyes. She was not looking at him but instead was studying Lady Amelia. Oliver felt his stomach twist, fearing something untoward was going to be said to Lady Amelia.

"This is Lady Alexandra," Lord Chadderfield replied, throwing a quick glance towards the young lady. "And her mother, Lady Spencer, is a short distance behind us—although she will reach us soon." He chuckled, making Lady Alexandra giggle, batting her eyelashes in Lord Chadderfield's direction. "And I would inquire as to your companion's name, but I believe we are both already fully aware of it." Again, he chuckled, but this time, in a somewhat unpleasant manner, making Oliver's skin prickle with disdain. "Lady Amelia, is it not?"

Lady Amelia inclined her head towards Lord Chadderfield and then towards Lady Alexandra, murmuring a short greeting. She said nothing more, but as she lifted her head, Oliver saw the pinkness in her cheeks and felt a slight stab of pain. Was this how she always felt when she was greeted by another member of the ton? Was she always afraid of what they would say? What they would think?

"We should continue our walk," he said, not wanting

Lord Chadderfield or Lady Alexandra to say anything to Lady Amelia that would embarrass her. "If you would excuse us."

"I must confess, I am surprised to hear you are courting Lady Amelia, Lord Montague," Lord Chadderfield said, taking a small sidestep to prevent Lady Amelia from moving forward. "I did not think such a lady would capture your interest."

Oliver bristled, a spurt of anger burning through his heart. "You may very well be surprised, Lord Chadderfield, but I can assure you Lady Amelia is the only lady in all of society who has ever captured my attention in such a profound manner," he stated, feeling Lady Amelia's hand tightening on his arm. "If you will excuse—"

"You will excuse my bluntness, Lady Amelia," Lord Chadderfield continued, interrupting Oliver, "but I must say, someone who has such difficulties as you do, Lady Amelia, could never once have thought Lord Montague would *ever* consider you!" He laughed as Lady Alexandra again began to giggle. "You must be blessed indeed, Lady Amelia—unless you have something over Lord Montague forcing him to stand by your side and insist all is well between you both and that he does, in fact, have a true regard for you."

"It is quite unbelievable, otherwise!" Lady Alexandra trilled, her eyes dancing with mirth as though Lady Amelia was worth nothing more than her mockery. "What is it that you have done to Lord Montague, Lady Amelia? Have you convinced him he needs your dowry? Has he made an agreement with your uncle whereby he will be given a great deal if he will only marry you?" She laughed again, as Lord Chadderfield continued to grin maliciously. "All of society is watching you with interest, Lady Amelia. I believe there are even some who are placing wagers on just how long such an interest will last."

"That is enough!"

Oliver had not meant to shout, had not meant to have his voice explode from his chest with such force that it shocked the smile from Lady Alexandra's face and the grin from Lord Chadderfield's lips. His rage had become so great, his anger over how Lady Amelia was being spoken to bursting through him with such force that he could not contain it any longer. His brows were low over his eyes, his hands clenched tightly together as he glared at Lord Chadderfield, who had now, at long last, finally lost some of the arrogance from his expression.

"That is enough," he said again, his voice much lower now but still holding as much severity as before. "How dare you speak to Lady Amelia in such a way? How dare you attempt to mock her? Attempt to ridicule her? Attempt to make her feel as though she is unworthy of being courted, of being noticed and of being appreciated, just as any other young lady might be?" He took a small step forward, with Lady Amelia's hand falling from his arm. "Do not think I will permit you to make such comments again, Lord Chadderfield," he finished, pressing one finger into Lord Chadderfield's chest. "The next time you choose to do so, there will be conse-quences." He did not speak of what such consequences might be but could tell from the flare of Lord Chadder-field's eyes that he did not need to do so. The gentleman was both taken aback and a little afraid of Oliver's threats. Oliver continued to stand directly in front of Lord Chadderfield, glaring down at him, until the quiet voice of Lady Amelia pulled him back.

"I believe Lady Smithton is approaching," she said, her voice calm and each word bringing an increasing sense of stillness to Oliver's anger. He turned to look at her, aware of how Lord Chadderfield immediately took a step back, whilst Lady Alexandra began to whisper furiously under her breath.

"Is she?" he asked, looking behind Lady Amelia and seeing how Lady Smithton was hastily coming towards them as though she knew something was afoot. She was accompanying Lady Amelia, of course, but had allowed them a few minutes to walk ahead and converse alone. Oliver frowned, seeing the dark expression on Lady Smithton's face and how her eyes narrowed as she glanced at him. Evidently, she had already decided he was entirely to blame. Giving Lady Amelia a quick smile, he then turned sharply back towards Lord Chadderfield and Lady Alexandra, his brows burrowing low.

"I do not think there is anything further to say, Chadderfield, save for your apology to Lady Amelia."

Lord Chadderfield, who had been on the point of turning around to take Lady Alexandra away from both Oliver and Lady Amelia, stopped dead and stared at Oliver, his mouth a little ajar. Perhaps he had expected to be able to get away from them without any further comment, but Oliver was not about to allow him to do so.

"Whatever is the matter?" he heard Lady Smithton

say, her breathing a little quickened as she came to stand by Lady Amelia. "Is there something wrong?"

"No," Oliver replied firmly, not looking away from Lord Chadderfield for even a moment for fear the fellow would scurry away. "It is only that we are waiting now for Lord Chadderfield and Lady Alexandra to apologize to Lady Amelia."

There was a momentary silence.

"Apologize?" Lady Smithton queried, sounding confused. "What was said?"

Oliver looked behind him, straight into Lady Smithton's face, his stomach twisting this way and that. He knew full well he was nothing more than a hypocrite, insisting Lord Chadderfield apologize for his rudeness towards Lady Amelia when he himself was guilty of a far worse crime. Despite that, however, Oliver was not about to allow Lord Chadderfield away from Lady Amelia's presence without apologizing for what had been said. He was angry about how she had been treated, furious as to how easily they had mocked her. It was as though they cared nothing for their own behavior, did not even give a flicker of a thought as to how Lady Amelia might feel about their harsh words.

"It does not bear repeating, Lady Smithton," he told the lady, seeing how she moved a fraction closer to Lady Amelia, clearly wanting to protect her. "But needless to say, it was cruel, unnecessary, and entirely unacceptable." His voice grew louder as he turned back to see Lord Chadderfield drop his head, perhaps now a little ashamed of what he had done, given that now Lady Smithton was also present and hearing of what had occurred. "Lord Chadderfield, Lady Alexandra." He spread his hand out towards Lady Amelia, expectantly.

It took some moment but, in the end, Lord Chadderfield sighed, shuffled his feet, cleared his throat, and then darted a quick glance towards Lady Amelia before lowering his head again.

"I apologize, Lady Amelia, for speaking without consideration," he said, his voice so quiet, Oliver could barely make it out. "It was uncalled for."

Oliver tipped his head just a little and looked into Lady Alexandra's face, seeing how she was looking from Lady Amelia to Lady Smithton and back again. Her face was pale, her eyes wide, and Oliver realized she was a little overcome with the fear of what Lady Smithton might say to others within the ton about what she had said to Lady Amelia. Lady Smithton held a high standing within society, and Oliver considered it quite correct for Lady Alexandra to feel so afraid.

"Lady Alexandra," he murmured, seeing how the lady's eyes darted to his, before dropping to the ground. Her cheeks began to color as she murmured an apology, which Lady Amelia accepted with a nod.

"Then I think there is nothing else to keep you both here," he said as Lord Chadderfield's jaw worked furiously, his brows knitting together in evident anger. "Good afternoon, Lord Chadderfield, Lady Alexandra. I do hope such a meeting will *never* happen again." So saying, he turned about and offered Lady Amelia his arm, seeing how she accepted it at once, without even a modicum of hesitation. Her eyes were warm as she gave him a quick smile, making something akin to satisfaction and contentment fill Oliver's chest. He led her away from Lord Chadderfield and Lady Alexandra, with Lady Smithton following close behind. Glad Lady Amelia did not walk with a downcast look on her face but rather with a small, gentle smile, and a slight lift to her chin, Oliver let out a long, slow breath and let the last of the tension rattle out of him.

"That was very good of you, Lord Montague," Lady Amelia said, her hand tightening on his arm for a moment. "You did not need to do any of that."

"But I did," he insisted, turning his head to look down at her and seeing just how her green eyes were fixed upon his own, searching them as though she might find a reason for his motivation within his steady gaze. "I had to ensure both Lady Alexandra and Lord Chadderfield knew you were not to be spoken to in such a manner, else they would continue to do so, and that is something I could not permit."

She gave him a small smile, her brows knitting for a moment. "A good many people speak to me as they did, Lord Montague," she answered, "but I have never had someone come to my defense in such a way as you. I cannot tell you just how much I appreciate your determination to stand up against such behavior on my behalf."

He came to a stop, resting his free hand onto hers as she held onto his arm. Aware Lady Smithton was walking only a few steps behind them, he took the opportunity to speak as honestly as he could.

"No one should be able to speak to you as they did, Lady Amelia," he told her, seeing how a faint color came into her face, how her eyes dropped to the ground for a moment as though she were a little embarrassed. "There is nothing about you that gives anyone any cause to be rude, ill-mannered, or inconsiderate. You do not deserve a single word of what Lord Chadderfield, Lady Alexandra, or other members of the ton say to you. It is they who are at fault, Lady Amelia, not you. You are quite without defect."

Much to his surprise, Lady Amelia began to blink rapidly, her eyes glistening with tears. He began to stammer, wondering if he had said something to upset her, only for Lady Amelia to place her other hand on to his and grasp his fingers.

"Thank you," she whispered, hoarsely, clearly a little overcome by all she felt. "No one has ever stood up for me before, Lord Montague, and I cannot tell you just how much I appreciate your determination to do so. Your kindness towards me speaks to my heart. I—"

She glanced to her left, seeing how Lady Smithton was now standing only a few paces away from them, clearly waiting until this conversation was at an end. Taking in a shuddering breath, she let go of his hand and looked up at him again, her lips in a tremulous smile. "I have always felt the ton look down upon me, that they mock me and tease me because of my limp. But you do not seem to see it. You only see...me." Pausing for a moment, she closed her eyes and let out a long breath, clearly gathering her composure. "That is both refreshing and quite wonderful, Lord Montague, for the time I have spent in London has been very trying indeed. Had it not been for Lady Smithton's kindness then I do not think I would have been able to stand the shame of the beau monde's inconsideration and mockery much longer." She sighed again, opened her eyes, and smiled at him, the tears gone completely now. "And you have brought a new brightness to my life, Lord Montague. In doing such a thing as demanding an apology for me, in showing Lord Chadderfield and Lady Alexandra that I am not unworthy of their respect, I feel my courage grow stronger. I finally feel as though, at least in your eyes, I am accepted."

Something came over his heart that Oliver could neither explain nor fully understand. It wrapped about his very soul and tore at his mind for, as he looked down into Lady Amelia's eyes, he felt something shift within him. There was a rapid warmth spreading through his chest and with it came the desire to tug Lady Amelia into his arms, to hold her tight against him, and to promise her he would always be present by her side, ready to defend her. He wanted to tell her she *was* accepted, just as she was, and that it was the beau monde who was at fault for treating her so cruelly, but the words stuck to his lips and would not remove themselves from him. His guilt began to weight him down, even as the desire to draw closer to her grew steadily. He was worse than Lord Chadderfield, was he not? He was courting Lady Amelia with his sole intention being that she would give him her heart. Thereafter, he was expected merely to step back and to continue along his path in life alone—but there was a growing desire within his heart for Lady Amelia to remain by his side, and for he to walk beside her.

"You are most welcome," he found himself saying, his throat rasping as he tried to speak encouragingly and without betraying any of the guilt he felt. "You are accepted in my eyes, Lady Amelia, and it is the fault of the ton if they treat you in any other way." Letting go of her hand and feeling immediately bereft, he cleared his throat, set his shoulders, and turned around, gesturing back towards the carriage, which stood some distance behind Lady Smithton. "Perhaps I should take you back to the carriage now."

"Yes," Lady Amelia sighed, throwing him a slightly rueful glance. "I am rather fatigued, in both body and spirit, Lord Montague, and would appreciate a chance to rest. Although," she finished, her voice softening again, "I am very grateful for your consideration."

Smiling at her, Oliver felt a heavy stab of guilt pierce his head, threatening to steal every single modicum of happiness battling for dominance within him. "But of course," he murmured, stepping forward and inclining his head towards Lady Smithton. "We are to return, Lady Smithton," he said by way of explanation. "It has been a little bit of a trying afternoon, and I believe we both might benefit from a restorative of some point."

"Tea, and perhaps whisky for Lord Montague," he heard Lady Amelia say, laughing as Lady Smithton's eyes narrowed just a fraction as she looked at him.

"But of course," Lady Smithton murmured, as they drew closer. "And mayhap you will explain precisely what occurred, Lady Amelia? It did seem to be an unfortunate incident."

Oliver cleared his throat. "It was, yes, but I believe it will not be repeated by Lord Chadderfield or Lady Alexandra," he said, feeling Lady Amelia squeeze his arm gently by way of thanks. "There is nothing particular to explain save to say Lady Alexandra and Lord Chadderfield thought they would be able to speak cruelly towards Lady Amelia, without any consideration for her. That way of thinking has been entirely removed from them now, I hope."

"I shall tell you everything the moment we are seated," Lady Amelia said, her voice filled with both relief and a touch of happiness. "But I will say this, Lady Smithton. Lord Montague stood up for me with such defiance and determination that I feel as though I owe him a great debt."

Lady Smithton looked surprised, coming to walk alongside Lady Amelia and glancing up at Oliver, who gave her a small, cursory smile before turning his gaze away.

"Is that so?" he heard Lady Smithton say, feeling a slight twinge of anxiety in his heart that she might, somehow, discover the truth behind his courtship of Lady Amelia. "Then I must admit I am a little surprised."

Oliver looked at Lady Smithton again, registering the considering look in her eyes as she watched him.

"But I am also grateful," she finished with a tiny smile in his direction, which Oliver grasped at without hesitation. "Thank you, Lord Montague, for what you did to protect Lady Amelia."

His guilt began to weigh down on his shoulders all the more as he nodded, smiled, and continued to walk towards the carriage without a word. He was more guilty of cruelty than either Lady Smithton or Lady Amelia knew, and yet here he was, pretending he was somehow better than Lord Chadderfield. His heart grew heavy, his shoulders slumping just a little. Lady Amelia would feel more pain and more sorrow over *his* betrayal, which was still to come, and then what would he do? Would he truly be content to walk away, to leave her with her pain and her humiliation? To leave her in the deepest darkness, lost in a fog of confusion and distress? Closing his eyes for a moment, Oliver let out a shuddering breath, feeling his heart begin to ache terribly. This was never once what he had intended when it came to Lady Amelia. To be forced into agreeing to a wager was one thing, but to be slowly trying to work his way into Lady Amelia's heart was quite another.

But he could see no way out. If he did not do as Lord Davidson demanded, then he would face the wrath of Lord Thornhill. But to continue with the bet would be to break Lady Amelia's spirit in a way more dreadful and more terrible than anything the ton had thus far been able to do.

Was he truly that cruel? That cold-hearted? Oliver could not answer such questions, feeling utterly wretched as he handed up Lady Amelia and then Lady Smithton into the carriage. He was quite broken, lost in confusion and fear and with no one to speak to, no one to turn to save for his troubled mind.

CHAPTER TEN

*A*melia sighed contentedly to herself as she looked at her reflection in the mirror. She was doing her level best to appear just as presentable as she could, but whilst the gown and the dressing of her hair were quite lovely, it could not account for the sparkle in her eyes.

That, she knew, came from her acquaintance with Lord Montague and the gentle care and consideration he had shown her over the last fortnight. When she had been presented with the cruelty of Lord Chadderfield and Lady Alexandra some days ago, he had been right by her side, refusing to allow them to continue their harsh, shaming words. She had been quite overcome by his determination to defend her, by his sheer force of will when it came to seeking and demanding an apology for her. In the days that followed, she and Lady Smithton had spoken often about what had occurred, with Mrs. Peters interjecting her thoughts on the matter, and on Lord Montague also.

It was very confusing, indeed. The more time she spent with Lord Montague, the more she found herself considering him in a very agreeable light. And thus, she found herself faced with the very same problem as before. Her regard for Lord Montague was growing so very steadily that she found herself almost desperate to be in his company. He called on her every day, and they had dined together three times—although with other guests also, of course. There had been a friendship struck up between them unlike anything she had ever experienced. Lord Montague was utterly charming, and she often found herself blushing at his compliments. Of course, she knew this might very well come from his plentiful experience when it came to encouraging a lady's attention, but she also knew he had not sought to court any of the other young ladies he had set his eyes on. She was the only one thus far he had sought out in that way.

"You look quite lovely, Lady Amelia."

Tugged out of her thoughts, Amelia turned to see Mrs. Peters standing in the doorway, looking at her affectionately.

"I thank you," she murmured, looking down at her gown and running her hands down the front of it. It was a deeper green than she had ever worn before, but the seamstress had been quite determined that this was the color Amelia should wear. Yes, it was darker than other debutantes might wear, but it would be striking, she had said. It would make people notice her, make them see the beauty of her eyes and face.

Amelia had not cared what the ton would think of her gown, nor what they would think of her eyes. Instead, she had found herself thinking only of Lord Montague, wondering what his reaction would be to her appearance and praying it would be a favorable one.

"You will catch his attention, Lady Amelia, have no fear about that."

Amelia blushed furiously, walking towards Mrs. Peters carefully, trying to ignore the pain in her leg but being grateful for Mrs. Peters supporting arm, which was offered the moment she reached her companion. "Lord Montague's attentions give me a great deal of courage," she told Mrs. Peters as they made their way to the staircase. "And much more boldness, might I say. I was always so very aware of the ton's watchful eye, how they would stare at me and whisper about me without hesitation."

"And now?" Mrs. Peters asked as they began to descend. "Lord Montague has encouraged you *not* to think of the beau monde in such a way?"

Amelia hesitated, walking carefully down the staircase and trying to ignore the stabbing pain that came with each step. "I—I do not think he has explicitly encouraged me to do so, no," she answered, letting out a breath of relief as she reached the bottom of the staircase, glad for the footman who stepped forward to take her arm so as to steady her. "But his very presence has encouraged me to do so. The fact that he does not look down on me and has come to my defense already makes me feel as though I ought not to care one jot about what the beau monde might think of me. He is quite right to state that my limp has no bearing on my character. It is the beau monde who is at fault for considering me in such an ill light, not my own."

"Of course it is not your fault!" Mrs. Peters exclaimed, looking up at Amelia in horror. "You cannot for a moment think that."

"I have, for a long time," Amelia admitted, quietly. "I felt as though my limp was a consequence of disobeying both my father and my governess and I should bear the shame and humiliation that came from the ton without complaint. I have found their cruelty almost unbearable, fearing I would be without friends and without a single suitor. I feared I would be left as a spinster, battling through the years alone. And then, you introduced me to Lady Smithton." She smiled at Mrs. Peters before accepting the hand of yet another footman as he helped her up into the carriage. "If it had not been for you, Mrs. Peters, I do not think I should ever have found myself in such a happy position as I do now. Lady Smithton was the very first to encourage me, to come alongside me and to help protect me from the viciousness of those about me. Lord Montague has continued that in his way, and I have found his attentions to be both a wonder and an encouragement to my spirits."

Mrs. Peters nodded slowly as she sat opposite Amelia, her face hidden in shadow as the carriage rolled away.

"I see," she murmured in a contemplative voice. "And what think you of Lord Montague now, Lady Amelia?" There was a short pause, a moment of hesitation. "I know you think very well of him now and I must ask—"

"I want to believe Lord Montague is everything he appears to be," Amelia interrupted, wanting to be honest with her companion but still refusing to admit to Mrs.

Peters the truth about what she felt for him. "He is charming, kind, helpful, determined, and more than considerate of me. In that regard, I find him to be..." She trailed off, struggling to find the right words to express how she felt. The carriage rolled on in silence, leaving Amelia rattling through her mind in an attempt to tell Mrs. Peters as much as she could without revealing her heart. "I find he is very amiable indeed," she finished lamely, knowing this was not the truth of the matter but feeling as though this was the correct thing to say. "I want to be in his company very often and truly enjoy every moment we are together."

"That is to be expected," Mrs. Peters answered with her voice still filled with a little uncertainty. "He has been very kind to you, and I will admit has impressed me with his behavior. There has never been a single moment when he has attempted to pull you from either myself or Lady Smithton."

"No," Amelia agreed, softly. "There has not."

"But that does not mean you should not remain on your guard," Mrs. Peters replied swiftly. "There may be more here than you know."

Amelia bristled, her sudden determination to defend Lord Montague surprising her with just how swiftly it filled her. "Or there might be nothing to your concerns, Mrs. Peters. It may be that, for whatever reason, he has changed his ways and decided I am worth his time. Mayhap he has seen society in the same way I have and has realized just how cruel it can be."

Silence met her words as Amelia subsided back into her seat, the fierceness of her determination washing away from her fairly quickly. She had surprised Mrs. Peters, she knew, but she had also astonished herself. Did she truly feel that strongly about Lord Montague? Did she honestly believe there was nothing but good in him now and that all the rumors and behaviors of the past had gone from him in a single moment?

Why should I not believe it? she asked herself, clasping her hands tightly together in her lap. *I have had nothing but kindness from him. He has defended me and treated me with such consideration that I could not help but think well of him. Neither has he ever attempted to encourage me to behave improperly, as Lady Smithton feared he might. Little wonder, then, that I wish to defend him!*

"Just tread carefully, Lady Amelia," Mrs. Peters said quietly as the carriage drew up to Viscount Harrington's townhouse, where this evening's ball was to be held. "Recall how, only a fortnight ago, you were afraid he might prove to be nothing more than a cad. Do not give up that wariness entirely."

Amelia did not reply, turning her head away and looking towards the door expectantly. Suddenly, she wanted to flee from the carriage, wanted to escape from Mrs. Peters and her pertinent remarks. She was happy, she realized. Happy for the very first time, given how society had treated her. Lord Montague had brought that into her life, had stood by her side and had brought her up out of her shame and her embarrassment to prove to her that not everyone saw only her limp and nothing more. Even the pain in her leg had seemed to lessen over the last few days as though his presence alone had brought a partial healing to her. And now that she had found such happiness, Amelia did not want anything to take it from her, did not want it to be stolen away by doubt or fear. Could she not trust he felt everything he said? He stated he saw her as he did every other young lady, that he found her strength and courage to be more than admirable. When he smiled at her, she found warmth and contentment in his eyes. Was she to mar that with an expectation that he would turn out to be nothing but a cad? Everything in her rebelled against the idea, perhaps fearing that if she began to question him, then she might never again be given the opportunity to be courted by another gentleman. Even though Lady Smithton had introduced her to other gentlemen who had been amicable and very welcoming, none had made any attempt to pursue her further. Just because she was being courted by Lord Montague did not mean other gentlemen could not seek her interest, but none had done so. That was not Lady Smithton's fault, of course, but Amelia could not pretend there were others who might seek her out should Lord Montague prove to be false in his supposed attentions.

"Here we are, then." Mrs. Peters sounded slightly strained, but Amelia did not allow herself to feel any regret for how sharply she had spoken. To her own mind, she was justified entirely in speaking as she had done, and it was with relief that she stepped out of the carriage and made her way slowly into Lord Harrington's townhouse.

"You waltz very well, indeed, Lady Amelia."

Amelia knew she was blushing, but she did not drop her gaze nor look away from Lord Montague, feeling very aware of the scrutiny that came from the others watching her. She had not danced at all as yet, which made this her very first foray onto the floor.

"I think you are doing well to support me," she answered honestly. "I know I must be a little less nimble than some of your other partners, Lord Montague."

He smiled, his eyes twinkling down at her. "That is where you are quite mistaken, Lady Amelia," he answered, making sure to keep the middle of the dance floor where they might move about more carefully and were less inclined to be knocked into by another couple. "You think much too little of yourself."

Feeling her cheeks heat a little more at his compliment, Amelia looked away, unable to keep his gaze and finding the emotions flickering in his eyes to be a bit too intense for her heart. She was no longer afraid of what the ton thought of her, not when Lord Montague had her in his arms. She was safe here, protected. No one would dare say anything to her when he was with her. News of how he had spoken to Lord Chadderfield had, of course, been threaded through all of society and now no one dared draw near her and speak in a similarly mocking or condescending manner—and for that, she was truly grateful.

As it has been with Lady Smithton, said a small voice in her head, reminding her Lady Smithton had been the first to come to her aid, had been the very first to step out with her into society, shielding her from the very worst of the *ton*. Amelia felt a twinge of shame, knowing she was being a trifle ungrateful and inconsiderate herself when it came to considering Lord Montague and not holding Lady Smithton in the same light.

"You look troubled," Lord Montague commented, appearing a little concerned as the dance came to an end. He bowed, still holding onto her hand, whilst she curtsied —and immediately felt a twinge of pain in her leg. "Does your leg pain you?"

"A little," Amelia replied honestly, having no inclination to hide such a thing from him. "But it is nothing."

"Here," he said, stepping forward and offering her his arm. "Allow me to return you to Mrs. Peters."

Amelia nodded, accepting his arm gratefully, leaning on him a little more as her leg grew weary. She needed to sit down and rest, and somehow, Lord Montague seemed to be aware of that without her informing him of such a thing, for he took her directly to a chair and helped her to sit down carefully.

"I cannot see Mrs. Peters nor Lady Smithton," he murmured, looking a trifle concerned. "Mrs. Peters was here but a few minutes ago, was she not?"

Amelia nodded, having to admit she was a little surprised to see Mrs. Peters was not exactly where Amelia had left her. Mrs. Peters never strayed from Amelia's side, which meant it was very odd indeed to see no sight of her now.

"I—I would go in search of her," Lord Montague said, looking a little awkward, "but I do not want to leave you here alone, Lady Amelia."

Amelia smiled up at him, grateful for his concern. "I

shall be quite all right," she said, knowing she needed to rest for a few minutes longer. "I know everyone will be looking at me and discussing my dancing, but I shall simply sit here quietly."

He shook his head, his eyes flickering. "You do not need to even consider what any other gentleman or lady here thinks of you, my dear Lady Amelia," he said firmly, bringing a warmth to her heart with his sweetness. "You were quite delightful, and I feel greatly honored in taking you to the dance floor."

She smiled, her heart aching with a furious affection that seemed to course all through her. "You are very kind, Lord Montague," she murmured, wondering just how she was ever to express to Lady Smithton or to Mrs. Peters the truth of what she now felt for Lord Montague. "But I fear I cannot help you when it comes to seeking out Mrs. Peters, for I have very little idea as to where she might have gone."

"It is most unusual," Lord Montague agreed, his brows lowering and a slight irritation playing about his mouth. "Perhaps she has just gone in search of some refreshments." Seeming to make up his mind, he nodded and set his shoulders. "I will wait with you for a few minutes, in the hope that she will return with all swiftness."

However, the few minutes they waited did not produce the results Amelia had expected. Mrs. Peters did not appear, and as hard as both she and Lord Montague looked about the room, neither of them could see either Mrs. Peters or Lady Smithton. It was most unusual, and Amelia began to feel a trifle anxious. Surely Mrs. Peters would not have left the ballroom, upset by what Amelia had said to her on the way to the ball? Yes, she had spoken honestly and with a good deal more harshness than she had intended, but there had been nothing within her speech that could have injured Mrs. Peters in a dreadful fashion. So where, then, had she gone?

"Good evening, Lord Montague."

Amelia frowned as she saw Lord Montague's expression darken at once, his entire frame seeming to tense, for his shoulders lifted and his jaw tightened, with his eyes narrowing as the gentleman who had greeted him drew closer.

"Lord Davidson," she heard him say, turning her head away so that she would not appear to be listening to their conversation. "Good evening."

"You were dancing with Lady Amelia it seems," Lord Davidson said in a cheerful tone. "It is the talk of society, of course."

Amelia closed her eyes, feeling a needling of embarrassment and have to force it away from her. She knew dancing with Lord Montague would send tongues wagging but, as Lord Montague had reminded her only a few minutes previously, she did not need to concern herself with what others thought of her.

"I was, and I hope to do so again," Lord Montague replied. "Now, if you will excuse me, I must go in search of Mrs. Peters or Lady Smithton." He turned away, meaning to go back towards Amelia, who had risen out of her chair, only for Lord Davidson to put out one hand to stop him.

"Lady Smithton, you say?" he asked nonchalantly,

giving Amelia a quick smile. "I saw her walking with another lady—fair-haired and slight—out in the gardens. Lord Harrington has an excellent display out there this evening. Lanterns of all kinds and some beautiful arrangements of flowers and the like, lit up by the lanterns glow. It is quite lovely, of course."

Amelia frowned, finding it very unusual indeed that Mrs. Peters and Lady Smithton would have left her sitting here alone with Lord Montague when they knew she was only dancing the one dance with him. "And you are quite certain you saw Lady Smithton there?" she asked as Lord Montague shook his head sharply. "You could not be mistaken?"

Lord Davidson laughed a little unpleasantly, and Amelia felt a slight shudder run through her as though instinctively, she knew this fellow was not a kind man.

"Everyone is well aware of who Lady Smithton is, so there could be no mistaking it," he answered, looking at her as though she were being idiotic. "Yes, I saw her there only a few minutes ago. I am certain she will return to you soon."

Amelia managed a tight smile and took Lord Montague's arm, thanking Lord Davidson but feeling the urge to escape from his presence just as soon as she could. "We should go to the gardens to find them," she murmured as Lord Montague began to walk slowly through the crowd of guests. "I do not understand why they have gone from the ballroom, but I fear it may be because of something I said to Mrs. Peters earlier today."

Lord Montague stiffened, turning to her and letting go of her hand. "No, Lady Amelia," he said firmly, his expression stern. "I will not lead you out of doors into the gardens. That is not what my intention is."

She blinked at him in surprise, opening her mouth to speak to him, only for him to catch her hand and place it on his arm, walking towards the open French doors leading to the gardens, going directly in contradiction to what he had said.

"We will linger near the door, but I will not step outside with you," he stated, moving towards the wall of the ballroom, where the shadows were thick and heavy. "But you must understand, Lady Amelia, I will not even consider risking your reputation by stepping out of doors with you. That is entirely improper and I—"

"Lord Montague, please!" Amelia clutched at his arm with both hands as they stopped together, looking up earnestly into his face and wanting desperately to impress upon him the truth that she did not think he would ever do so. "It would not be improper by any means! There are many guests going in and out of those doors, and the gardens are clearly so well-lit, there is no opportunity for impropriety. Look!" Catching sight of Lady Alexandra walking alongside another gentleman out into the gardens, she gestured to them pointedly. "You have too much concern for my safety, Lord Montague," she finished, looking up into his face as he turned back to her. "Can you not see I trust you?"

These words seemed to bring him more pain than relief. He lowered his head, rubbing one hand over his forehead, murmuring something she could not quite make out. Alarmed by his apparent upset, Amelia pressed one hand gently to his arm, feeling as though she ought to be giving him some comfort, even though she did not know why he appeared so ill at ease.

"You should not trust me, Lady Amelia."

Lord Montague's voice was harsh and rasping, his features contorted as he looked up at her, shaking his head as he did so. "You should not give me even a modicum of your trust."

"But why should I not?" Amelia asked, a little breathlessly. "I know of your reputation, Lord Montague, and you know very well that, from the beginning, I have not been certain of this courtship. But now that I have spent more time with you, now that I have seen how you defend me to your peers, how can I not begin to trust you have changed? That you may, in fact, be the gentleman no one ever believed you would become?" Taking a small step closer to him, she looked up into his eyes, her heart hurting for him as she saw the confusion in his eyes. "You fear yourself, Lord Montague. You fear you may yet be dishonorable. Mayhap you are afraid of what you have begun to feel." Ignoring the jolt of anxiety that crashed through her as she spoke, Amelia swallowed hard and forced herself to continue. "Surely you cannot be unaware of how my feelings have changed towards you these last two weeks, Lord Montague," she whispered, unable to hold his gaze any longer as she told him more than she had ever intended. "You have defended me, have encouraged me, and have made me feel more than I ever imagined I could feel." Her voice grew quieter still, her heart beginning to race as he touched her hand with his, making her look up at him once more. "I confess I have been confused with what I feel for you, Lord Montague. I have tried to battle it, particularly when Lady Smithton and Mrs. Peters have told me to ensure you are not to be trusted. I have wanted to stay away from you so that my regard for you will not grow any further, but neither of my desires have been achieved. And now," she finished, seeing how Lord Montague's eyes darkened with emotion, "I find I do not want my heart to give up what it now holds for you."

"Stop, Lady Amelia, please."

Her heart swirled in her chest. She had been about to state she cared for him deeply, about to confess that she loved him, but he had prevented her from doing so by a mere word. Lord Montague said nothing for some moments, leaving Amelia standing on the edge of a precipice. Either he would tell her he had no feelings at all and did not understand what she spoke of, or he would admit to her that she spoke the truth. Blood roared in her ears as Lord Montague sighed heavily, closing his eyes and shaking his head as though he was struggling with what he was to say to her in response.

"Lady Amelia, you must not say anything more."

Lord Montague opened his eyes, moving just a fraction closer to her. The sound of the guests near to them began to fade away, the music from the orchestra becoming nothing but silence. All Amelia could hear was her breath, waiting desperately for Lord Montague to say something further.

"You are much too good for someone such as me."

His voice was filled with tenderness, his hand reaching out and brushing her cheek with such a gentleness that Amelia wanted to lean into him, her eyes filling with tears of happiness.

"You speak of things with such honesty that I find myself wanting to do the very same," he continued, his hand running from her cheek to her shoulder and down her arm until his fingers twined with hers, making her heart cry with joy. "I will not hide the truth from you, Lady Amelia." Again, he sighed, closing his eyes tightly and wincing as he did so. "I am the very cad you think me."

Her happiness evaporated in a moment. She froze, her body weighted as she stared up at him, not understanding what he meant. Had she been entirely wrong? Had he been pretending to feel something for her? Had he felt nothing at all and had only come to her defense so as to make her enamored towards him?

"I never intended to have such an affection for you, Amelia," he whispered, opening his eyes and gazing down into her face. "I did not think I would be so affected, but I know now I cannot leave your side. My waking hours are spent wishing to be near you. My heart longs to hear your voice, to know what you have to say, to do my utmost to make you smile. And yet, I have hidden that from my very self, trying to convince myself that what I felt meant nothing. But," he continued, swallowing hard and taking in a long breath. "But I have found myself just as you describe—with a deep regard for you that will not leave me but instead continues to grow, filling me until I cannot deny its presence."

Amelia did not mean to cry, but a single tear streaked down her cheek as she tried to take in what Lord

Montague had said. He had called himself a cad because he had been hiding his feelings from her and had not spoken to her of what was in his heart. That, as far as she thought, did not make him so, but apparently, to his mind, that was precisely what he was.

"Pray, do not cry," he whispered, looking utterly wretched. "Oh, Lady Amelia, what is it I have done?"

She swallowed her tears and wiped the one from her cheek, feeling her lips curving up into a smile as she realized the truth. Lord Montague cared for her, just as she cared for him. Her fears and her doubts, and the fears and doubts of Lady Smithton and Mrs. Peters were to come to naught. Lord Montague's reputation would not be carried into her future. Things were about to change.

"I think I have fallen in love with you, Lady Amelia," she heard him whisper, staring up at him in disbelief as those words fell from his lips. "I cannot explain it, cannot understand it, but I fear I have reached a place from which I shall never be able to return."

Amelia closed her eyes so that her tears would not fall from her lashes, feeling herself practically burst with joy. Her heart echoed his, but she could not find the words to express it, such was her happiness. If she spoke, then she feared she might break down completely, losing her composure entirely and catching the attention of the guests nearby who, thus far, had not even cast a single glance in their direction.

"I—I cannot do this any longer."

Opening her eyes, Amelia was astonished to see Lord Montague now looked entirely ill at ease. Instead of the same joy she felt being expressed in his eyes, he appeared to be becoming more and more distraught. His eyes were wild, darting from place to place, and he began to shift from foot to foot. Pressing her hand for another moment, he let it go and took a step back as though to leave her entirely.

"I must go," he said hurriedly, turning away from her only to come back to her side and take her hand again. "Oh, Amelia, I will confess to you now that all that is said of me is entirely true. I am everything you think me to be. Everything Lady Smithton said about my character is beyond doubt. They were right to warn you from me. I am the worst sort of gentleman, and yet I am a gentleman who has come to love you with all that I am. My arrogance and selfishness have been revealed to me, tearing aside my flesh and revealing the darkness that lingers in my heart. And that is all because of you, Amelia. It is *all* because of you." Shaking his head, he lifted her hand and pressed his lips to it for a long moment, sending a shiver up her arm. She did not know what he meant by what he was saying, feeling almost numb with confusion. "I speak the truth when I tell you I love you, Amelia. I love you desperately, and if I were sure you would agree, I would ask you to become my wife." Her heart leaped in her chest, only for her to realize Lord Montague was *not*, in fact, about to ask her that wonderful question.

"Why would I refuse you?" she asked, her voice barely louder than a whisper. "I do not understand."

"I know," he answered, looking more pained than she had ever seen him. "I know you do not understand, but in the days to come, I am sure you will." Letting go of her hand, he took a step back, a finality in his expression that frightened her. "Know, Lady Amelia, I am deeply, deeply sorry for all that will come. I was only thinking of myself and the consequences that might follow. I did not truly consider you until I realized you were more wonderful, more beautiful, and more inspiring than any other lady of my acquaintance. And now, it is too late." He spread his hands, his voice filled with hopelessness. "I have lost everything. I am so very sorry, Amelia. Despite it all, know I have come to feel for you a love that will endure for the rest of my days." Turning away from her, he pressed one hand to his heart as though he were trying to prevent it from breaking. "Goodbye, Lady Amelia."

CHAPTER ELEVEN

Oliver wanted to ride away from London, ensconce himself in his estate and hide away until his heart no longer screamed at him with both guilt and pain. Speaking to Lady Amelia last evening had broken every single part of him. He had known his heart had begun to care deeply for the lady but had never once considered what it would be like to hear her speak of her affection for him. When she had begun, he had felt the first stab of shame lance through his heart, which was followed by another, and then another, until he felt as if he might crumple to the floor in agony.

It was an agony of his own making, of course. An agony he could not blame anyone else for. Lord Davidson had made the bet, yes, but had he not grown too close to Lady Thornhill in the first place, then there would have been nothing Lord Davidson could have used against him. Had he never become this arrogant, selfish, pig-headed rogue, then he might now have found a contented happiness with Lady Amelia, might well have seen the beauty that she was long before now. Perhaps she would never have had to endure the mockery of the *ton*. Perhaps she would never have needed to struggle in the way she did at present.

The foolishness of his heart and the idiocy of his actions hit him time and time again, making him want to lose himself in the hazy fog of too much brandy, too much liquor. Then, perhaps, he might forget—at least for a time —the foolishness of what he had done.

Lady Amelia would know about his bet soon enough. Lord Davidson coming to speak to him last evening, in Lady Amelia's presence, had been warning enough. It was a reminder that Lord Davidson was watching him, that he was making certain Oliver was close to fulfilling his bet so that Lord Thornhill would not have to be told of his wife's indiscretions, and so that Lord Davidson might make enough money to pull him out of his current debts.

And now, the only way to turn his back on it all was to go to Lord Thornhill himself and to state what he had done. Even though it had been during last season, Oliver knew the consequences for him when it came to telling the truth might be severe indeed. Lord Thornhill held a good deal of influence. He could make quite sure Oliver was thrown from society, that he was rejected by almost everyone he knew. There would be no return from that. It could take years before he was welcomed back to London—and he certainly would never enjoy the same privileges as he did at present.

But somehow, when he considered Lady Amelia, he knew such things did not matter. Whether society rejected him or not, all he cared about was Lady Amelia. He ached for her. It was not until last evening, when she had spoken the truths of her heart to him and suggested he too might be struggling with some of his own feelings, that he had come to realize the full extent of his affections. It was love. It could have no other explanation. The desire to be near her almost every hour, every minute. The eagerness with which he counted the seconds until he could be in her company once more. The way his heart lifted when he saw her approaching, his joy in their conversation, and how much he delighted in hearing her laugh. The anger that rose within him when someone spoke to her disparagingly, growing within him the need to protect her. It all amounted to one thing— love. He loved Lady Amelia, and now he was to separate from her for good. There was no hope for him now, not when she discovered the truth. She would be heartbroken over what he had done, realize he had deliberately meant to deceive her, and even though he now found himself in love with her, his assurance of his devotion would not take away the pain of his betrayal. His shame would be his torment.

"Another brandy, my lord?"

He looked up to see a footman handing him another glass, which Oliver accepted with a mutter of thanks.

"And Lord Havisham wishes to join you," the footman added, just as Oliver saw the tall, broad-shouldered, and rather angry looking Lord Havisham approaching from across the room. Oliver had no time to rise from his chair, no time to escape from the fury that was Lord Havisham and could only scrabble at the arms of his chair with one hand, afraid Lord Havisham was about to plant him a facer.

"Montague."

Lord Havisham stood directly in front of Oliver's chair, his eyes narrowed with anger.

"Lord Havisham," Oliver murmured, his heart pounding furiously, recalling Lord Havisham was very close to Lady Smithton. "Good evening."

Lord Havisham let out a long breath, his jaw jutting forward. "You have brought much pain to Lady Amelia, Montague. I do not understand why, and neither, I fear, does she."

Oliver closed his eyes and let out a long breath, a cold hand grasping at his heart. "I—I think she will come to understand it very soon," he said hoarsely. "All will discover it, Lord Havisham. I have made a dreadful mess of things, and I must set them aright before Lord Davidson wins his wager." Realizing what he had said, he opened his eyes to see Lord Havisham staring at him, his brows lowering slowly. "I will not pretend," Oliver continued, lifting his brandy to his mouth and taking a sip in the hope that it would give him a little more courage, "I did not want to take on this wager, Lord Havisham, but I had no other choice. Lord Davidson threatened to reveal something that would ruin me and have me thrown from society, and initially, I considered such a consequence too great for me to endure." Another sip of brandy sent a flare of warmth through him, chasing away a little of the cold that had seemed to settle in his very bones. "I now know such consequences mean nothing."

Lord Havisham let out a long breath, his jaw working furiously, only for him to stalk past Oliver and walk directly towards the betting book. Oliver sat dully in his chair, thinking that no matter what Lord Havisham's reaction was, he deserved everything that would come to him. Finishing his brandy, he set the glass down on a small table to his left and sank back. He shouldn't drink anymore, he decided. He would not be able to manage the rest of the evening if he had too much liquor running through his veins.

"What is the meaning of this?"

Lord Havisham rounded on him, standing closer than before and his breathing quick and fast.

"What is it you have done, Lord Montague?" he hissed, his eyes narrowing all the more. "Explain yourself."

Oliver nodded, a sigh leaving his lips. "It is as I have said, Lord Havisham," he muttered, darkly. "I have been pursuing Lady Amelia in the hope that I might succeed in having her speak to me of her heart. Then Lord Davidson will win the wager and, given a few gentlemen have wagered that I will *not* be able to do so, he will win a substantial amount of money. It also means Lord Davidson will not reveal to Lord Thornhill that I was much too close to his wife last season." He heard Lord Havinsham catch his breath, knowing the mention of the Marquess of Thornhill had quite astonished the fellow. Evidently, Lord Havisham was fully aware of the man's reputation and standing within society.

"You are stating, then, that Lord Davidson black-mailed you," Lord Havisham murmured, seemingly growing a little less angry and sinking into a chair near to Oliver's. "That is why you accepted the wager?"

"I felt I did not have a choice," Oliver answered, honestly. "But I did, Lord Havisham. This is not something I wish to blame others for. I could have refused Lord Davidson entirely; I could have faced the consequences of my prior actions. But I did not." He shrugged, shaking his head. "But now I intend to do so."

Lord Havisham blinked, leaning forward in his chair and looking at Oliver with sharp eyes. "You mean to say you are going to speak to Lord Thornhill?"

"I am," Oliver answered miserably. "I can see no other way to ensure Lord Davidson is unsuccessful, nor to prove to Lady Amelia that I have no intention of going through with my plan." He looked up and saw Lord Havisham studying him, his eyes a little narrowed still. "I love her. I love her desperately, and now I must separate from her, for otherwise, I will break her heart completely."

"I fear you have done so already," Lord Havisham muttered, pushing one hand through his hair. "I do not know what to think, Montague. I do not want to believe you but given what you have said and given your countenance at the present moment, I think I have no other choice but to do so."

Oliver shrugged again, having no particular concern as to whether or not Lord Havisham believed him. If Lord Havisham intended to bring down consequences upon his head for what he had done to Lady Amelia, then Oliver would accept them without hesitation or question. Otherwise, Lord Havisham could believe what he wished.

"I do not want to help you," Lord Havisham grated, his expression darkening. "But I feel as though I have minimal choice but to do so. Not for your sake, of course, but for the sake of Lady Amelia."

"No."

Oliver half rose from his seat, pointing one hand out towards Lord Havisham. "No, you cannot. You *must* not."

"She cares for you."

"I do not deserve her!"

This shout rang out across Whites, making almost every other gentleman pause in their conversation, turning to look at who might have been making such a ridiculous noise. Oliver sank back down in his chair, covering his face with his hands and wishing to heaven that Lord Havisham had never come in search of him.

"I do not deserve her," he said again, dropping his hands to his lap and looking morosely at Lord Havisham. "I know she has come to care for me, but I will not use that against her. Her heart must forget me, Lord Havisham. I am not worthy of her affections." Swallowing hard, he sighed heavily again. "You *know* what I have done, Lord Havisham. You know I am a selfish, arrogant, cruel man. Why then would you wish for Lady Amelia to tie herself to me?"

A glimmer of a smile crossed Lord Havisham's face. "Because," he said, leaning forward and fixing Oliver with his gaze. "Because you have proven to me, Lord Montague, that you are truly in love with Lady Amelia.

You would not be as distraught as you are at present if you were not. You are willing to give her up entirely, to be without her for the rest of your life, all so she will be protected from you. That speaks of an affection that runs deeply through your heart. And besides which..." He trailed off, looking all about him for a moment, looking a little desperate. "You are not the only gentleman who has made a foolish mistake," he said eventually, his expression grim. "I made a catastrophic mess of things some years ago. I must hope she will see the evidence of my regard for her, of my change of heart, and be willing to give me another opportunity to prove myself to her."

Oliver frowned, not quite certain of whom Lord Havisham spoke, but wondering to himself whether the gentleman referred to Lady Smithton.

"You must give Lady Amelia the choice as to whether or not she can give you even a modicum of trust," Lord Havisham continued, earnestly. "Once she has become aware of the truth, aware of everything you have done and everything you regret, she may then decide to give you another opportunity to prove yourself."

"And if she does not?"

Lord Havisham sighed and sat back in his chair, his eyes growing a little sorrowful. "There is always the possibility she will do that," he admitted, quietly. "But even if there is the smallest flicker of hope that Lady Amelia might give you another chance, Lord Havisham, then do you not wish to pursue it?"

Oliver considered this for some moments. He could not feel hope at this present time. There was not an ounce of expectation in his heart, nothing but darkness and dismay. A vision of Lady Amelia laughing up at him, her emerald eyes gleaming with delight, began to burn into his memory. He had managed to make her laugh once, had managed to bring her joy. Was he now to have that only as a memory, never to see it again? Or was there the smallest chance he might be able to see her so contented once more?

"I think it only the remotest chance such a thing will occur," he said honestly. "And yet I feel such a longing in my heart that I cannot turn away from it." With weary eyes, he looked back at Lord Havisham, who was nodding with a grim sense of determination in his expression. "I just do not know what I am to do to express to her the desires that linger within my heart."

Lord Havisham's eyes flickered. "You say you intend to speak to Lord Thornhill?" he asked as Oliver nodded. "You plan to tell him all that occurred between yourself and his wife?"

"I do," Oliver answered, his stomach twisting with a sudden nervousness, knowing full well what Lord Thornhill's reaction would be. "I must remove the opportunity for Lord Davidson to blackmail me by ensuring Lord Thornhill knows all." He swallowed hard and lowered his gaze. "No matter what the consequences will be."

There was a short silence. Oliver stared down at the ground miserably, still feeling as though Lady Amelia would reject him entirely when it came to the truth of the matter. He might profess his love, fall on his knees and beg for her forgiveness, but he was still quite certain the pain he had brought her would be too much for her to bear and certainly too much to forgive.

"I know Lord Thornhill," Lord Havisham said slowly, breaking into Oliver's thoughts. "Allow me to arrange the meeting on your behalf."

Oliver opened his mouth to ask why, only for Lord Havisham to hold up one hand, continuing to speak.

"Lord Thornhill is, as you know, a very particular man. He may not agree to your calling upon him and may also refuse an invitation from you."

Oliver sighed and nodded miserably, knowing full well his reputation preceded him and that someone like Lord Thornhill might choose to stay clear of his company.

"Therefore, I shall have him call upon me," Lord Havisham continued, firmly. "And you will be present also when he arrives. Do you concur, Lord Montague?"

Not truly understanding why Lord Havisham was showing such willingness and desire to help him, Oliver studied the gentleman for a few minutes. Lord Havisham's eyes were steady, his jaw set and a faint anger glistening in his eyes. Oliver knew he could not refuse such an offer, not when Lord Havisham was clearly doing all of this to aid Lady Amelia, and yet there was still reluctance to accept, fearing that it would all tumble down on his head.

"Lord Thornhill might cause a great disturbance, Lord Havisham," he muttered, passing one hand over his eyes. "But I can see you are willing to accept such a consequence, and I must express my gratitude to you." Sighing heavily, he rubbed one hand down his face and nodded. "I agree. I will come to your home whenever you wish it."

"Good," Lord Havisham replied, leaning forward in his chair as a resolute expression began to creep across his face. "And thereafter, perhaps the following day, I shall have you meet with Lady Amelia."

Oliver's heart began to beat furiously in his chest, his stomach twisting this way and that with the furious anxiety that beset him almost at once.

"It must be done," Lord Havisham continued, a trifle more gently as though he knew precisely what Oliver was feeling. "You shall have your opportunity, and Lady Amelia shall have hers. I shall ensure it, Lord Montague."

A sudden fear caught Oliver's heart, and he shook his head, firmly. He could not imagine Lady Amelia being brought into Lord Havisham's house, ready to meet with Oliver, only to discover the deep and terrible truth.

"No," he muttered, rubbing at his forehead and feeling a dull ache begin to settle there. "No, I cannot permit her to meet with me without her knowing the truth, Lord Havisham. That is unfair." He looked up and saw Lord Havisham frown. "I shall write to her," he continued, pinching the bridge of his nose in an attempt to ward off his aching head. "I must write to her to express all I feel and all I have done." The truth he could put into words, could write down on a page instead of struggling to find the words to tell her all he had done. "Once she has read it, once she knows the truth, then she can decide whether or not she wishes to meet with me, Lord Havisham." He dropped his hand and looked directly at the gentleman, seeing how his expression cleared, and his eyes filled with understanding. "That, I think, is only right."

Lord Havisham's mouth lifted in a half-smile. "Again, you prove your true consideration for her, Lord Montague," he murmured, a little quietly. "But yes, you are quite correct. That *would* be best. Therefore, if you write to her, then I shall ensure the letter is placed into her hands."

Oliver nodded quickly, having nothing else to say. He could not argue, could not pretend this was not what he wanted. "Very well," he agreed, quietly. "I thank you, Lord Havisham." Swallowing hard and thinking he might need another brandy, Oliver gestured to a footman, pointing to his empty glass. "And when might such a meeting be, Lord Havisham?"

"In two days hence," Lord Havisham answered, swiftly. "I shall make all the arrangements and will ensure you are kept abreast of any changes to my plans."

Oliver nodded, taking the glass of brandy from the footman gratefully and sitting back a little more in his chair. The weight of his responsibility had not left him and nor had the awareness of his guilt. Lady Amelia would soon know everything—and then, what sorrow would be hers!

Sorrow that was entirely his own doing. His heart filled with shame once more as he brought the glass of brandy to his lips, drinking deeply. Whatever conse-quences would come, he would accept them with open arms. He was nothing more than a fool, nothing more than a selfish rogue who had cared nothing for anyone but himself.

And it was time Lady Amelia knew that.

CHAPTER TWELVE

"*I* do not understand."

Amelia could feel tears beginning to creep into the corners of her eyes but refused to allow them to fall. She blinked them back hastily, just as Mrs. Peters pulled out a lace handkerchief and handed it to her.

"You want me to read this?"

"It is from Lord Montague," Lord Havisham explained, handing the letter to Amelia. "He has much to explain."

Amelia winced, knowing full well Lord Havisham was aware of just how much torment Amelia had endured of late, given Lord Montague had behaved in such a confusing fashion. Reaching up, she took the letter from him, studying the writing on the front.

It merely said, 'Lady Amelia.' That was all. The seal on the back was Lord Montague's, and he had been the one to pen her name on the front. The weight of what was contained within began to burden her heart, making her confusion begin to rise within her all over again. Her head grew heavy, and she set the letter down in her lap, refusing to study it any longer.

"You are not going to read it now?" Lady Smithton asked, looking at her from across the room. "You have no urgency to find the explanation for his strange actions?"

Amelia lifted her chin, a little surprised at how Lady Smithton had spoken. "I shall read it when I am alone," she stated, firmly, aware of how Lady Smithton's cheeks colored. "I have no desire to do so at present."

"But of course," Mrs. Peters interrupted, putting one hand on Amelia's arm. "That is quite understandable."

Lady Smithton rose to her feet abruptly, her color high. Walking across the room, she strode to the window and looked out at the scene below, keeping her back to Amelia and Mrs. Peters. Amelia said nothing, a little confused at Lady Smithton's behavior but also determined not to open her letter from Lord Montague.

"I am sorry, Lady Amelia."

Surprised, Amelia turned her head to see Lady Smithton still looking out of the window, her voice quiet.

"I should not have asked you such a thing," Lady Smithton continued, sounding somewhat tired. "I confess I am very confused as to Lord Montague's behavior, and I feel as though I have been more of a hindrance than a help to you." She turned slowly, looking at Amelia with a grave expression. "You came to me with the request that I help you, and I fear I have been entirely unable to do so. Lord Montague's reputation went before him, of course, but given he has confessed his heart to you, I find myself greatly confused by his actions. I do not know what advice to give you, Lady Amelia."

Amelia managed a small smile, seeing the frustration in Lady Smithton's eyes. "I do not think ill of you, Lady Smithton," she promised, honestly. "You tried to protect me from Lord Montague, tried to warn me away from his attentions, and yet my heart refused to listen." A warmth spread across her face, matching the warm regard in her heart as she spoke of Lord Montague, seeing how Lady Smithton nodded. "I confess to you now I have long been struggling with my feelings for Lord Montague, Lady Smithton. I did not want to heed your advice but forced myself to do so—and yet, I found my affection for him continued to grow." Her eyes began to burn with tears again, her throat aching painfully. "When he spoke to me of his own regard, I felt such joy, I could barely breathe. My heart began to sing with happiness, my whole being filled with such delight that it was as though I had been transported to heaven." A single tear dropped from her eye, but Amelia immediately dashed it away. "When he turned from me, when he stated he could no longer continue with our courtship, I felt such an agony that it was as though my heart was being torn from my chest, as though my soul was being pulled from my body." She swallowed hard, refusing to let any more tears fall. "And that pain has not left me as yet."

Mrs. Peters pressed the handkerchief to Amelia's hands, and she took it with a grateful yet wobbly smile.

"I am truly grateful to you, Lady Smithton," she finished, seeing the lady shake her head. "You have done your best to guide me, but my heart has been unwilling to give up its affection. I find myself more in love with Lord Montague than ever before, even though he has stepped away from me." Glancing down at the letter, she shook her head sadly. "Mayhap that is why I do not wish to read this letter, for then I fear it will reveal a truth to my heart I can never recover from."

Lord Havisham cleared his throat and took a small step forward, drawing Amelia's attention. "I must tell you, Lady Amelia, I know the truth of the matter." He waited for a moment as though he wanted to allow her time to absorb this. "And Lord Montague's heart is as he states it to be. He does care for you, Lady Amelia. In fact, I believe he has the deepest of affections for you. However," he continued, making her heart sink to the floor, "there is much you must know first, before your heart can make its choice." Hesitating for a moment, he glanced towards Lady Smithton, who was looking as uncertain as Amelia felt. "Come to my residence, Lady Amelia. Tomorrow. At four o'clock precisely."

Amelia blinked in surprise, glancing at Mrs. Peters, who was looking quite astonished. "Tomorrow?"

"Tomorrow," he stated, quite firmly. "You must be on time. Lady Smithton, you will accompany her, I hope? As well as you, Mrs. Peters."

Both ladies nodded at once, leaving Amelia feeling as though she were being swept along without having any firm understanding of where she was going or why her presence was being requested.

"I think you will be grateful for my eagerness in this, once you fully understand it all," Lord Havisham explained, not giving any clarity to what he meant. "Read the letter when you will, Lady Amelia, but regardless of what you feel, you must attend tomorrow." His brows knitted together, as a dark expression flickered across his face. "Lord Montague does not deserve your kindness nor your willingness nor, even, your forgiveness, but I suspect a heart of love will find a way to do so in the end." A glimmer of a smile crossed his face as he glanced towards Lady Smithton. "A deep affection can cover all manner of sins."

Amelia saw Lady Smithton turn her head away, a troubled look in her eyes. The letter burned her fingers, making her look down at it again. What was it Lord Montague had written? What truth did Lord Havisham now know that he feared would turn her from Lord Montague altogether? Her heart began to beat hard against her chest as a swirl of anxiety rushed through her.

"You will come tomorrow, Lady Amelia?"

She looked up from her letter, seeing Lord Havisham's concerned expression. "I—I will," she agreed, quietly.

"Even if what you read in the letter turns you away from the idea entirely? Even if you feel as though you do not wish to be with anyone save for your own company?" There was a slight hardness to Lord Havisham's tone as though he were concerned her word would not be enough.

Amelia nodded, her eyes narrowing just a little as she looked back at Lord Havisham. "You have my word," she stated, as Mrs. Peters nodded. "I will be at your residence tomorrow, Lord Havisham. At four o'clock precisely."

∼

It was some hours later before Amelia had a chance to sit alone with Lord Montague's letter. She had spent some time with Lord Havisham, Lady Smithton, Mrs. Peters, and, latterly, the other members of 'The Spinster's Guild' who had joined Lady Smithton for dinner. There had been a slight strain between Lady Smithton and Lord Havisham, she had noted, which she had found a little troubling. Where it founded from, she could not say, but the quick glances between them and the somewhat stilted conversation made it quite apparent there was something yet unsaid that needed to be spoken of between the two.

The dinner had been a welcome distraction from all that was going on within her own heart, Amelia reflected, as she thanked the maid before sending her from the room. She had been able to laugh, to smile and to enjoy the conversation between the other ladies of 'The Spinster's Guild' and had felt a surge of hope with the news that one, Miss Bavidge, had managed to find herself a very respectable gentleman and was, in fact, now engaged! The letter from Lord Montague had remained almost entirely forgotten as she had shared in Miss Bavidge's joy, glad for the lady that she had found such happiness.

And now, some hours later, she was entirely alone and now ready to read the letter Lord Montague had written her. Lord Havisham had given her fair warning that there were to be truths within it that would pain her, but she had already given her word that she would be present at Lord Havisham's home tomorrow afternoon, regardless of what she read.

"Oh, Lord Montague," she whispered, feeling the

same surge of pain within her heart that had come to her the very first moment he had stepped away from her, leaving her only with that faint impression of his lips on her hand and a hope that had immediately begun to die away. "What is it you have done?"

She pressed the letter to her chest, closing her eyes tightly and feeling the bite of curiosity press into her heart. It had been such a wonderful moment, to share with Lord Montague the love that had been within her heart. She had known then that he did not see her as so many others did. They looked at her limp and then at her, in her entirety, whereas he saw only her. Her limp meant nothing to him. He did not disregard her because of it, did not treat her cruelly or mock her over it. Instead, he had found in her a beauty she had barely been able to see herself. He had encouraged her, helped her, brought her forward into the light and refused to allow her to escape back into the darkness. He had defended her to others, had refused to let his peers speak to her in the way they thought she deserved. In short, he had shown her the evidence of his love without even speaking a word of it to her.

Tears began to cloud her vision, and Amelia blinked rapidly, forcing them away. Her hands shook as she turned the letter over and snapped the seal apart. Unfolding it, she looked it over carefully, her heart racing furiously.

"My dear Lady Amelia," she read aloud, her voice nothing more than a whisper. "You will think me a fool, a rogue, and a cad, for that is what I am. I will not shirk from it. And yet, my heart has found a love for you that

*will never be removed from me. Your name is etched there,
ever to remain, even though I know I do not deserve your
affections in return. I am unworthy of you, Lady Amelia,
for I have done you a most cruel wrong."*

Her hand pressed to her mouth as she continued to
read, no longer able to whisper the words aloud. Her
vision blurred; her heart began to ache with such a heavy
pain that it was all she could do to continue reading. Lord
Davidson had made a bet, and Lord Montague had
agreed to it. He had agreed to it due to his own
cowardice, his fear—of that, he freely admitted. There
was no pretense there, no unwillingness to face the truth.
Over and over, he told her he was entirely at fault,
entirely to blame. At first, he had thought only to ensure
the bet was won and that he would escape without any
difficulty, only to find himself in love with her. His heart
had built up such a regard for her that he had not known
what to do.

Amelia wanted to scream aloud, such was the agony
within her heart. Lord Montague had played her for a
fool, and yet within his conniving, there had come a
strange affection he had not been able to explain. He had
tried to turn from it, just as she had done, but it would not
allow him to depart.

But she had not been sought out by him, as she had
first thought. He had not come near to her due to his own,
honest interest. He had done so in order to encourage her
affections, to get her to fall in love with him so that he
might win the bet and be freed from any threat of Lord
Davidson's.

Her heart burned with a fierce pain that stole her

breath. She wanted to cry out aloud but knew she could not do so, for fear of rousing the staff or her uncle. Tears streamed down her face as she sobbed, the letter now lying on the bed beside her, the final few words left unread. Lord Montague was right to state she would now see him as nothing more than a rogue and a cad. Everything he had called himself, she could not pretend she did not agree with. He had taken her affections and attempted to use them against her, had tried to toy with her heart, but instead had found his own caught up in much the same way as hers.

Her whole body shook with agony and sorrow. Curling up into a ball on her bed, Amelia pulled the covers over herself, her eyes sore with tears. Lord Montague had betrayed her. Nothing of what he had said, nothing of what he had done, had been honest. His singular desire had been to protect himself from the consequences of what might come should Lord Davidson carry out his threat. He had not cared for her.

But he has told you the truth now, said a small voice within her. *He has confessed all to you because of what he now feels. Are you to turn away from him altogether?*

She could not answer that question, for the pain within her heart was much too great to be reckoned with. Everything in her wanted to remove herself entirely from Lord Montague, feeling the trust she had allowed herself to have in him had now been shredded completely. She did not know Lord Montague, she realized, not in any true sense. She could not tell whether what they shared had been with the true Lord Montague or with a character he had played in order to encourage her affections. The times he had stood by her side, had come to her defense and had encouraged her to ignore the dark, malicious glances of the *ton*—had that been nothing more than Lord Montague play acting the gentleman he knew she needed? Or had he truly felt the anger, the frustration and the urge to defend her? Could she trust now that anything he said was, in fact, the truth? Did he really care for her? Was this affection, this regard, truly within his heart?

What if, in writing this letter, he seeks to have you confess your love for him regardless? Would that not prove to both himself and Lord Davidson, that you have, in fact, fallen in love with him? Love forgives, does it not? It is unrelenting, even in the face of great pain and great wrongdoing. If you write to him, if you go to him and tell him your heart is still filled with none but him, then will he not declare himself the victor?

Closing her eyes, Amelia covered her face with her hands, feeling her confusion and her doubts beginning to swirl all around her like dark shadows. She did not know what to think and certainly did not know what to do. Lord Montague could not be trusted, for his words might be very easily twisted to have her do what was required for him to win his bet. Lord Davidson might be forcing him to prove she loved Lord Montague so that his bet could be won in its entirety.

"What do I do?" she whispered, her body beginning to shake as she sobbed into her pillow. The letter fell to the floor, the final few lines still unread, as Amelia began to cry in earnest. Her leg ached terribly, reminding her of its presence, of the strife it had caused her. Her heart was sore, her mind filled with agonized thoughts, and her whole being burning with a mixture of shame and humiliation.

What was she to do? She had given her word, yes, that she would go to Lord Havisham's home tomorrow afternoon, but everything within her rebelled against the idea of even leaving the house. She wanted to stay here, hidden away, lingering in sorrow until the pain began to lessen just a little. Why had Lord Havisham been so insistent? Why had he urged her to give her word?

Soon, a quietness began to take a hold of Amelia's heart and mind. A quietness that came after a long bout of weeping, sending a weariness through her that she could not ignore. Her eyes began to close, her questions remaining unanswered, but such was her weariness that she could not give them any more of her strength. A few more tears streaked down her cheeks, soaking into her already damp pillow. Lord Montague had taken her for a fool, and she had proven him correct in his estimation of her. She had given him her heart easily, finding she was so desperate to be accepted just as she was that she had allowed her heart to fill with him without much hesitation. Yes, Lady Smithton had warned her from him, and yes, she had tried her best to take heed of such concerns, but she had been quite unable to prevent her affections from growing. In the end, she had been glad to give her heart to him, had been overjoyed to share with him the regard that now lingered with her—and he had promised her that he too felt the same, only to turn his back on her completely.

Amelia took in a ragged breath, her eyes closing

tightly. She did not know what to think now, and certainly did not know what to do. When the morning light came, perhaps she would be able to see things a little more clearly, but for the moment, she would have to linger in her sea of confusion and pain. Sleep would hold no peace for her, she was quite certain, for her dreams would be filled with none but him.

"What am I do to?" she whispered aloud, pulling the covers around herself a little more tightly before, finally, she drifted off into an uneasy sleep.

∾

"My dear Lady Amelia!"

Amelia held up one hand as Lady Smithton threatened to swoop down to her, her concern evident in her expression.

"I am quite all right, Lady Smithton, I assure you," she said, knowing full well her white face and red-rimmed eyes portrayed precisely the opposite. "I thank you."

Lady Smithton blinked, then looked to Mrs. Peters, who gave a small shake of her head.

"Lord Havisham has explained all to me," Lady Smithton murmured, gesturing for Amelia to come further into Lord Havisham's small parlor, where there was a tea tray waiting. "I am very sorry to hear of what Lord Montague has done, Lady Amelia."

Amelia said nothing but sat down quickly, feeling a sudden weakness in her limbs she wanted desperately to fight. Ever since she had risen this morning, she had felt herself so tired and weary, it was taking every ounce of her strength merely to continue this conversation. She was numb now, feeling as though her heart had been pulled from her and nothing but an empty space now sitting in her chest.

"It was a great shock," she murmured as Mrs. Peters pressed a cup of tea into Amelia's cold hands. "I did not once imagine I was nothing more than a plaything to Lord Montague." She turned her head away, not wanting to give in to the tears that threatened yet again. "It has been a difficult truth to accept, Lady Smithton, as I am sure you understand."

"And yet," Lady Smithton said quietly, her eyes searching Amelia's face as Amelia looked back at her. "There is a small modicum of hope, is there not?"

"Hope?" Amelia spat the word back at her. "There is no hope. Lord Montague only wrote to me in the hope that I would still confess my love for him, that I would tell him that despite it all, I cannot pretend I do not feel an affection for him."

Mrs. Peters' eyes widened as she looked back at Amelia, clearly startled. "But for what reason, Amelia?" she asked as Amelia closed her eyes against the fresh wave of tears that threatened. "His letter appeared to be quite genuine."

"Do you not see?" Amelia whispered, hopelessly. "He intends to have me do as Lord Davidson has stated. If I tell him my heart is filled still with regard for him, that will prove to Lord Montague *and* to Lord Davidson that I love him desperately. Lord Montague will win the bet. Lord Davidson will gain his coffers, and Lord

Montague will be freed from any fear that Lord Thornhill will know of his indiscretions."

There was silence for a minute or so, with both Mrs. Peters and Lady Smithton exchanging troubled glances. Amelia said nothing more, turning her head away from them both and feeling her heart sink low in her chest. She did not know precisely why Lord Havisham had asked her here this afternoon, but nor did she truly care. There was too much of a burden on her shoulders, too much sorrow and sadness that crushed her, breaking both her spirit and her heart.

"You do not believe his words, then," Lady Smithton said softly. "That is not something I shall condemn you for, Lady Amelia. It is more than understandable. But," she continued, leaning a little forward in her chair, "I must ask you whether or not you do truly love Lord Montague still, as you have just said."

Amelia sighed heavily, closing her eyes and forcing herself to nod, knowing she was unable to force the words from her lips. Even through the pain and the sorrow, she knew the love she had for Lord Montague had not gone from her heart. It had faded a little, of course, torn down by the agony of his actions, but she had not lost it entirely. Just quite how long it would take for her to remove it from herself, she did not know, but she prayed it would not be overly long.

"Then I shall continue to give you my words of guidance," Lady Smithton said gently, her expression filled with compassion. "I confess I fear I have not been the help I ought to have been to you, Lady Amelia, but I shall state what I feel regardless." She smiled gently, but

Amelia felt no hope nor comfort, dropping her gaze to the floor. "I still cling to the belief that there may yet be a modicum of hope, Lady Amelia. Lord Montague has done you a great disservice, yes, but he may be truthful in his repentance. I can well understand your reasons for disbelieving him, but I shall pray for a moment of hope that spreads out towards a future happiness, Lady Amelia. That is, after all, what we are present here for this afternoon."

Amelia lifted her head sharply, looking directly into Lady Smithton's face and seeing the glimmer of a smile on the lady's face. "Why am I here, Lady Smithton?" she asked, feeling a trifle uneasy. "And why has Lord Havisham not yet come to greet us?"

Lady Smithton opened her mouth to explain, only for the sound of voices to reach Amelia's ears. Looking around the room for some explanation as to where these voices now came from, Amelia's eyes finally found the source of the noise. A door to the right of the fireplace was now a little ajar. She had not noticed it before, having come in an entirely different way.

"Lord Montague has called upon Lord Havisham," Lady Smithton explained quietly, getting to her feet and creeping towards the door, where Amelia noticed three chairs had been placed. "And Lord Thornhill is expected at any moment."

Amelia caught her breath, staring wide-eyed at Lady Smithton, who was now beckoning her towards the door. Swallowing the lump in her throat, she began to shake her head, her whole body caught up with a sudden shudder. "I cannot," she whispered, a wave catching her and throwing her about with the fury of her emotions. "It would not be right."

"Normally, I would advise you most severely that eavesdropping is not at all seemly," Mrs. Peters murmured, leaning towards Amelia and pressing one hand atop hers. "But in this situation, my dear lady, I know it would bring you a good deal of clarity, which would aid you in your struggles."

"Clarity?" Amelia repeated, not quite certain what Mrs. Peters meant and still quite overcome with what Lady Smithton was asking her to do. "I am to listen to a private conversation in the hope that it will bring me some sort of understanding?"

Mrs. Peters smiled gently. "But of course," she answered, pressing Amelia's hand. "You state you believe Lord Montague wrote you such a letter in the hope that you would still profess your love so that he might win his bet. What if that is not so? What if he means every word?"

Amelia shook her head, her throat beginning to ache. "I cannot know that."

"But you *can* know it," Mrs. Peters said pointedly. "Lord Montague is about to meet with Lord Thornhill. Does that in itself not tell you something about his letter? About his true desires?" She patted Amelia's hand again and then sat back, her gaze firm. "Listen to what is said and allow the truth of it to enter your heart. Then you will know for certain whether or not Lord Montague has meant what he said to you in his letter. You will have no doubts when it comes to his statement of affections for you." She smiled as Amelia let out a long breath, her shoulders settling as she realized what Mrs. Peters and Lady Smithton meant. "There is, as Lady Smithton stated, still a modicum of hope. If he proves to be true in his affections and if you can find a forgiveness for him within your heart, then there may be a happy future awaiting you, Lady Amelia. And whilst I do not condone what he did, I know a heart filled with love is more than many a young lady has been able to hope for."

Amelia's throat worked furiously as she blinked back tears. She had been quite determined that everything Lord Montague had said in his letter had been solely for his own purposes, for his own desires. She had convinced herself his words meant nothing and they were said only to encourage her affections. But now, it seemed, she was being given the opportunity to discover whether or not it was the truth.

"I—I do not know what to do," she whispered as Lady Smithton moved back towards her, graceful as ever. "What if he does not do as you both seem to expect?"

"Then you will feel a great deal of pain," Lady Smithton replied without hesitation. "I would not pretend to you that it will be easy to endure, Lady Amelia, but I must admit, I do not believe it will be as you fear." Holding Amelia's gaze, steadily, Lady Smithton gestured towards the door. "Lord Havisham met Lord Montague in Whites. Lord Montague spoke to him there, told him he had every intention of speaking to Lord Thornhill so that Lord Davidson could have no hold over him any longer. Lord Havisham then insisted on arranging the meeting here, so you, Lady Amelia, might be able to know the truth. The fact that Lord Montague has appeared, just as he stated he would, gives the impression he is just as willing as before to state the truth to Lord Thornhill."

Amelia sucked in a breath, her stomach tightening. "But he will be punished severely," she whispered, realizing the enormity of what Lord Montague was about to do. "Lord Thornhill will bring down grave consequences upon his head—although I will not state they are not deserved." She swallowed hard, seeing Lady Smithton nod in agreement. If Lord Montague has truly willing to speak to Lord Thornhill, to admit his fault, and thereby remove Lord Davidson's hold on him, then Amelia would have to admit she had been mistaken about his motivations to write to her in such a way. All she had to do was to rise to her feet, walk across the room, and sit down so that she could overhear the conversations.

A third, louder voice echoed from the room next to the parlor, making Lady Smithton look round.

"You must decide, Lady Amelia," she said urgently, looking back at Amelia quickly. "It seems Lord Thornhill has arrived."

Amelia took in a long breath, steadying her composure. Her heart began to quicken as she got to her feet, her chin lifting a little as she nodded to Lady Smithton.

"I will listen," she said softly. "But what I shall do thereafter, I cannot say."

Lady Smithton smiled and beckoned her towards the other side of the room. "Then come," she murmured as Mrs. Peters rose to her feet to join them. "And let us listen together."

CHAPTER THIRTEEN

*O*liver could not remember an occasion when he had felt like this. His palms were sweaty, his throat feeling like sandpaper, and his voice a little hoarse as he greeted Lord Thornhill. Moisture beaded on his forehead as Lord Havisham gestured for both gentlemen to sit down.

Licking his lips, he grunted his thanks as Lord Havisham handed him a glass of whisky, knowing full well he would need a good deal of courage to speak as openly and as honestly as he was about to. In his mind, he allowed himself to remember Lady Amelia, knowing he was doing this because of her. She had come into his life in a most unexpected fashion, even though he had never intended to have her invade almost every part of his heart and mind. Had he never met her, had he never forced himself towards her, then he might now be continuing as the rogue he had always been. He had a good deal to thank Lady Amelia for, even if she would never belong to him in the way he had once hoped. He could now go forward, even with the consequences Lord Thornhill was sure to bring, knowing his life had forever been changed.

"Lord Montague," Lord Thornhill muttered, observing Oliver with a shrewd eye. "I did not expect you to be present this afternoon."

Oliver cleared his throat before taking a small sip of whisky. Lord Thornhill, being an older gentleman, had a good deal of gravitas about him. There was a presence that filled the room, leaving Oliver with the uncomfortable impression that Lord Thornhill might already be aware of the reasons for this strange meeting.

"I did intend to call upon you myself," he began, irritated with himself that his voice was so hoarse. "But Lord Havisham suggested it might be easier if a meeting was arranged at his townhouse."

Lord Thornhill eyed Lord Havisham for a moment before returning a quizzical eye to Oliver. "And what you mean by that is Lord Havisham did not believe I would be willing to meet with you, Lord Montague," he said, betraying his sharp and calculating mind. "To which, I state, he would have been quite correct." His brow lowered, his lips pulling tight for a moment as he eyed Oliver. "You are not the sort of gentleman I would ever wish to have in my acquaintance."

Oliver winced, looking away from Lord Thornhill as the hard truth hit him square between the brows. "I can well understand that," he stated, honestly, not quite looking at Lord Thornhill. "I confess now I have turned from that way of living, Lord Thornhill, but there are things I must still do to ensure I have set my back to it completely."

"Oh?" Lord Thornhill lifted one eyebrow, eyeing Oliver carefully. "And what is it you wish to say to me?"

Oliver hesitated, his throat closing as everything in him began to scream a warning. If he told Lord Thornhill the truth, then the consequences that might follow could be unbearable. He would not be able to hold his head up in society for years to come.

And yet, he knew he had to tell the gentleman the truth. Lady Amelia meant so much to him that he could not allow Lord Davidson to have a chance of winning his bet. He had to tell Lord Thornhill what he had done.

"I am a rogue," he stated honestly, aware his voice was rough and feeling a tension rattle all through him. "I will not pretend otherwise, Lord Thornhill. My reputation is as such as I am aware that I have brought much shame to myself, which I fear I shall never be free from."

Lord Thornhill said nothing but merely took a sip of his brandy whilst Lord Havisham looked on, encouraging Oliver by his mere presence. Taking in another long breath, Oliver let it out slowly and tried to find the right words to say.

"I have often enjoyed the kisses of young debutantes but have never once pursued them further than that," he stated, fully aware such a thing was not, by any means, an accolade. "However, I have enjoyed the company of other ladies of the *ton*, who are able to share their affections without concern." This was, of course, an odd way of trying to state the truth, but Oliver did not want to blurt out that he had enjoyed a warm acquaintance with Lady Thornhill last season, for fear of what might occur thereafter. He was trying his best to put it in as careful a way as possible, in the hope that Lord Thornhill might be able to understand the truth without Oliver having to fully express it. "Most were wealthy and independent widows, whilst one or two of my acquaintances merely avoided their husbands." Cringing inwardly, he looked towards Lord Thornhill, seeing the man's expression darken and feeling quite certain the gentleman knew of what he was speaking. "These...acquaintances have now come to an end and have been over for at least a year or more, but I will not pretend they did not occur."

There was nothing but silence for some minutes. Lord Thornhill did not take his eyes off Oliver, whilst Lord Havisham swirled his drink in his glass but said nothing. The tension grew steadily, with the atmosphere darkening with every second that passed. It was as if a gathering storm had entered the townhouse, with dark clouds swirling above Oliver's head and a lightning bolt threatening to strike him at any moment. He could do nothing other than wait, seeing how Lord Thornhill's face was growing angrier with every moment that passed.

"You mean to tell me, Lord Montague, you have enjoyed a closeness with my wife?"

The question hung in the air for a moment, the answer burning on Oliver's lips. He could deny it, could pretend this was not at all what he had meant, but in doing so, it would only be to save his reputation. That was not the sort of gentleman he was any longer. He was not the arrogant, selfish cad he had once been.

"That is precisely what I am telling you," he said honestly. "I can only apologize, Lord Thornhill, for the trouble and the strife I have caused you."

Lord Thornhill's jaw worked furiously for a moment or two, his eyes narrowing all the more. "And might I ask why you are so eager to tell me this, Lord Montague?" he rasped, his hand white on the whisky glass. "Surely you must know I do not take such a slight lightly?"

Oliver nodded. "I am fully aware of what might follow," he said honestly. "I will not pretend I have not done wrong, Lord Thornhill, for my guilt is plain before me." Swallowing a quick mouthful of whisky, he drew in a long breath. "I tell you this so that the lady I care for will not bear any consequences for my foolish actions." Again, a vision of Lady Amelia came to his mind, and he found his determination bolstered. "I was foolish enough to be swayed by a gentleman who wanted to use my indiscretions against me. In short, I treated her most ill and, in doing so, realized just how cruel I have become." His head lowered as the weight of his sins bore down on him again, their fierceness biting at his heart. "I do not deserve the affections of that particular lady, and yet she gave them to me regardless. I will not permit her to be further used by this particular gentleman, nor by myself for that matter. Therefore, to ensure such a thing does not occur, I sought to confess the truth to you, Lord Thornhill."

Much to Oliver's surprise, Lord Thornhill let out a bark of laughter. Laughter that was filled with disbelief and mockery as opposed to mirth.

"Surely you cannot expect me to believe for one moment that you have any sort of true affection for a lady of the *ton*!" Lord Thornhill laughed, shaking his head.

"You are saying this only to encourage me not to punish you for what you have done!"

Oliver shook his head, feeling his heart sink into his boots. "I would try to convince you otherwise, Lord Thornhill, but I know very well my reputation does not do anything to encourage you to believe I am telling the truth."

"No," Lord Thornhill agreed, with a mocking smile. "It does not. I know you to be a manipulative, cruel sort who cares nothing for others and will use all manner of ways to get what you desire. Why, then, should I believe you now?"

There was no answer to this, Oliver knew. He could not defend himself. There was nothing he could say that would make Lord Thornhill believe him.

"If I might," Lord Havisham interrupted, making Oliver lift his head. "I would not have arranged this meeting, Lord Thornhill, unless I believed Lord Montague was genuine in his affections. There is a desire here to change, and I must support that, for the sake of the lady in question."

Lord Thornhill snorted in apparent disdain but made no further remark.

"I will accept whatever consequences you wish to throw at me," Oliver stated, quietly, seeing Lord Thornhill's eyes swivel back to him. "I accept them without hesitation nor protest. They are entirely what I deserve."

There was silence for some moments, but Oliver found a small sense of peace begin to fill him. He had done what he had sought to do and, in doing so, had found a release that he had not even known he needed.

There was nothing to tie him to Lord Davidson's will any longer and, with the letter he had written to Lady Amelia, she too would know the truth. His heart ached in knowing she would, most likely, turn away from him completely, but there came a contentment in knowing what he had done was the right thing.

"Lord Montague," Lord Thornhill grated, his expression still one of sheer fury. "I am not inclined to believe a word of what you say. You have done a great ill to my good name."

"I am ready to bear my shame," Oliver replied calmly. "I will return to my estate and will not come to London again."

Lord Thornhill shook his head, his lip curling. "I should call you out for it," he grated, harshly. "I should seek to pull your heart from your chest for the disgrace you have brought on me." He took in a long breath as if he were still deciding whether or not he ought to do such a thing. "But I shall not. I know full well you are not the only person to blame in this sordid circumstance."

Oliver leaned forward in his chair, looking at Lord Thornhill directly. "I was the one who encouraged your wife, Lord Thornhill," he said bluntly. "I will bear the entirety of the blame without hesitation."

Lord Thornhill held Oliver's gaze. "That may be so, but to speak aloud of what has occurred will only reveal the depths of my shame to all of society." He bit his lip and then glanced at Lord Havisham. "You say only one other gentleman is aware of what occurred?"

"Lord Davidson," Lord Havisham said without hesitation. "Yes, I believe so." He looked towards Oliver, who nodded, feeling a trifle confused. He had expected Lord Thornhill to do everything he could to shame and disgrace him for what he had done, but now it seemed Lord Thornhill was going to do all he could to hide Oliver's misdemeanors from the world.

"Then I shall speak to him," Lord Thornhill grated, turning back towards Oliver. "Although I must demand you do as you have stated, Lord Montague. I do not wish to see you within society for some time."

Oliver nodded, a wave of relief crashing over him. This was not at all what he had expected, given Lord Thornhill was known to be a hard man. "But of course."

Lord Thornhill rose to his feet, his expression still black with anger. "I will not say I appreciate your honesty, Lord Montague," he muttered, turning away from Oliver. "But I will state it has surprised me. Although I cannot believe you truly have an affection for a lady of the *ton*." He threw a dark glance towards Oliver, who rose to his feet also. "You simply did not wish Lord Davidson to hold this over you, I think."

"I care very deeply for her," Oliver replied with a great deal of firmness in his voice. "In fact, Lord Thornhill, I consider myself in love with her. I believe I have lost her entirely, however, given just how cruelly I have treated her, but I will never regret allowing my heart to open towards her. She has shown me what courage is, Lord Thornhill. She has endured a good deal of mockery from the *ton*, has seen their cruelty and their harshness, and has shown me my part in it. I have been forced to look at my own character and to see my failings there, staring back starkly at me." He shook his head, thinking of just how much he cared for Lady Amelia when he knew he was not worthy of her. "I love her deeply, Lord Thornhill, and will carry her within my heart for the rest of my days."

Just as Lord Thornhill was about to open his mouth, just as he was about to say something in response, a door to Oliver's left swung open. He had not even noticed the door before but, turning towards it, he was utterly astonished to see Lady Amelia now stood framed in the doorway. Her eyes were fixed on his, her face pale but a beautiful smile beginning to spread across her face.

"You have proven your love for me, Lord Montague," she whispered, her voice sounding like a thunderclap. "I did not want to believe it, I did not want to trust you, but now I see your heart is true."

He blinked rapidly, overcome with astonishment. Lady Amelia began to walk towards him slowly, her limp barely noticeable. She held her hands out to him, and it was all Oliver could do to lift his own, hardly able to believe it was she who now stood before him.

"You—you heard everything?" he asked hoarsely, not even noticing Mrs. Peters nor Lady Smithton walking into the room behind Lady Amelia. "I did not know you would be there."

She smiled up at him, her eyes glistening with tears. "Nor did I know you would be present," she answered, her fingers twining with his. "I felt such fear in reading your letter. I let myself believe it was just another ploy to win this bet, but now that I have heard you speak with such honesty to Lord Thornhill, I know now every word you wrote was the truth." A slight blush caught her cheeks. "You will not be angry with me for eavesdropping, I hope?"

Oliver could not speak, such was the lump in his throat. Looking down into Lady Amelia's face, he felt the desire to crush her against him grow steadily within him as though this would prove to him she was, in fact, truly standing before him.

"I think we shall retire to the parlor," Lady Smithton said, interrupting the otherwise silent room. "Lord Havisham, are you escorting Lord Thornhill to the door?"

In a few minutes, the room had emptied itself of Mrs. Peters, Lady Smithton, Lord Havisham, and Lord Thornhill, leaving Oliver standing alone with Lady Amelia. His heart began to race, his thoughts tumbling over each other as he fought to find the words to say.

And then, Lady Amelia leaned into him, her head resting on his chest and her hands loosening from his. There seemed to be nothing to say for the present moment, for Oliver could only wrap his arms about her waist and hold her close, feeling as though finally, in the midst of his darkness, there had come a small but beautiful light. Light that was none other than Lady Amelia.

EPILOGUE

*A*melia had never been this close to a gentleman before and yet, wrapped in Lord Montague's arms, it felt as though this was the only place she was meant to be. Hearing everything Lord Montague had said to Lord Thornhill had brought her out of her dark misery and into a fresh and wonderful hope that had filled her entire being until she had been quite unable to stay away from him any longer. Upon hearing his declaration of love, she had flung open the door and fixed her eyes upon his.

The surge of happiness that now ran through her chased every little bit of doubt and fear away. Lord Montague loved her. She loved him. He had turned his back on his previous way of living and had, instead, chosen to be an honest gentleman. He had given up everything to protect her, and she loved him all the more for it.

"I am not worthy of you, Amelia."

His voice was muffled, his words whispered into the nape of her neck.

"You have shown me your words and your devotion to me are true," she whispered back, closing her eyes as she wound her arms about his neck. "You told Lord Thornhill the truth so that Lord Davidson would have no hold upon you. You chose to turn your back on me so that I would not do as Lord Davidson had wagered I might." Opening her eyes, she lifted her gaze to his, seeing just how close his face was now to hers and feeling a thrill of anticipation run up her spine. "But how can I pretend I do not have a love for you when it has already taken over me?"

He smiled softly, his eyes filled with tenderness. "The bet will not be won," he whispered, gently. "I will tell all and sundry I confessed my love to you at the first. Therefore, Lord Davidson will not win his wager, and he shall have no hold over me any longer." Reaching down, he brushed his hand over her cheek before letting his fingers, with infinite gentleness, twine through her hair. "Although I fear, Lady Amelia, I must return to my estate and not think of returning to London for some years."

She laughed up at him, her heart lifting all the more. "You cannot think I will regret leaving London?" she asked him, teasingly. "The *ton* will not be something I ache to return to, Lord Montague, for it has never been my friend."

"No?"

"No," she replied, looking up into his eyes and feeling her whole being tingle with excited anticipation. "The only thing I have ached for is you, Lord Montague. You have shown me more kindness than any other of my acquaintance. You defended me. You have protected me. And now, I know you have done it all because of the love you have for me. I trust your words. I trust your heart. I have set the past behind me, knowing your regret for what you have done is real."

His hands dropped to her waist again, pulling her even closer than before.

"You are more than I have ever deserved," he breathed, his head lowering slowly. "Your kindness, your forgiveness, and your courage overwhelm me, my love." He paused for a moment as though he were summoning up the courage to speak honestly. "I want you as my wife, Amelia. I ask you to be my bride and to share my days with me, forever." His lips brushed hers, sending a spiral of heat right through her. "What do you say, my love? Can you give me not only your heart, but also your hand?"

She did not hesitate, happiness enveloping her completely. The past was forgotten already, broken down by the words she had heard him speak. There was no doubt left lingering in her mind, no fears capturing her heart. All that remained was her love for Lord Montague, a love which she knew was fully returned. Yes, he had made mistakes, but she would not linger on those, not when her future with him was now brighter than ever before.

"I will give you everything," she replied, reaching up to capture his face with her hands so that she might look intently into his eyes. "I love you desperately, Lord Montague. Yes, I will be your wife."

His smile spread across his face, making her laugh with joy. Then, his lips sought hers once more in a long, languorous kiss that sent ripples all through her, whilst her heart filled with more happiness than she thought it could contain. Love had captured their hearts in a most unexpected fashion, but it had tied them together for the rest of their days. Amelia could hardly wait for their life together to begin.

Have you read the Books 1-3 in the Spinsters Guild series?
A New Beginning
The Disgraced Bride
A Gentleman's Revenge

MY DEAR READER

Thank you for reading and supporting my books! I hope this story brought you some escape from the real world into the always captivating Regency world. A good story, especially one with a happy ending, just brightens your day and makes you feel good! If you enjoyed the book, would you leave a review on Amazon? Reviews are always appreciated.

Below is a complete list of all my books! Why not click and see if one of them can keep you entertained for a few hours?

The Duke's Daughters Series
The Duke's Daughters: A Sweet Regency Romance Boxset
A Rogue for a Lady
My Restless Earl
Rescued by an Earl
In the Arms of an Earl
The Reluctant Marquess (Prequel)

A Smithfield Market Regency Romance
The Smithfield Market Romances: A Sweet Regency
Romance Boxset
The Rogue's Flower
Saved by the Scoundrel
Mending the Duke
The Baron's Malady

The Returned Lords of Grosvenor Square
The Returned Lords of Grosvenor Square: A Regency
Romance Boxset
The Waiting Bride
The Long Return
The Duke's Saving Grace
A New Home for the Duke

The Spinsters Guild
A New Beginning
The Disgraced Bride
A Gentleman's Revenge
A Foolish Wager

Love and Christmas Wishes: Three Regency Romance
Novellas

Collections with other Regency Authors
Love, One Regency Spring
Love a Lord in Summer
Rogues Like It Hot

Please continue on to the next page for a preview of

the first book in The Spinsters Guild series, **A New Beginning**! If you have already read A New Beginning, please try The Returned Lords of Grosvenor Square: A Regency Romance Boxset. It will keep you entertained for hours!

Happy Reading!

All my love,

A SNEAK PEEK OF A NEW BEGINNING

CHAPTER ONE

"Good evening, Miss Taylor."

Miss Emily Taylor, daughter to the Viscount Chesterton, kept her gaze low to the ground, her stomach knotting. The gentleman who had greeted her was, at this present moment, looking at her with something akin to a leer, his balding head already gleaming in the candlelight.

"Good evening, Lord Smithton," she murmured, hearing the grunt from her father than indicated she should be doing more than simply acknowledging the gentleman's presence. The last thing Emily wished to do, however, was to encourage the man any further. He was, to her eyes, grotesque, and certainly not a suitable match for someone who had only recently made her debut, even *if* he was a Marquess.

"Emily is delighted to see you this evening," her father said, giving Emily a small push forward. "I am certain she will be glad to dance with you whenever you wish!"

Emily closed her eyes, resisting the urge to step back from the fellow, in the knowledge that should she do so, her father would make certain that consequences would follow. She could not bring herself to speak, almost feeling Lord Smithton's eyes roving over her form as she opened her eyes and kept her gaze low.

"You know very well that I would be more than pleased to accompany you to the floor," Lord Smithton said, his voice low and filled with apparent longing. Emily suppressed a shudder, forcing herself to put her hand out and let her dance card drop from her wrist. Lord Smithton, however, did not grasp her dance card but took her hand in his, making a gasp escape from her mouth. The swift intake of breath from behind her informed Emily that she was not alone in her surprise and shock, for her mother also was clearly very upset that Lord Smithton had behaved in such an improper fashion. Her father, however, said nothing and, in the silence that followed, allowed himself a small chuckle.

Emily wanted to weep. It was obvious that her father was not about to say a single word about Lord Smithton's improper behavior. Instead, it seemed he was encouraging it. Her heart ached with the sorrow that came from having a father who cared so little for her that he would allow impropriety in front of so many of the *beau monde*. Her reputation could be stained from such a thing, whispers spread about her, and yet her father would stand by and allow them to go about her without even a twinge of concern.

Most likely, this was because his intention was for Emily to wed Lord Smithton. It had been something

Emily had begun to suspect during these last two weeks, for Lord Smithton had been present at the same social gatherings as she had attended with her parents, and her father had always insisted that she greet him. Nothing had been said as yet, however, which came as something of a relief, but deep down, Emily feared that her father would simply announce one day that she was engaged to the old, leering Lord Smithton.

"Wonderful," Lord Smithton murmured, finally letting go of Emily's hand and grasping her dance card. "I see that you have no others as yet, Miss Taylor."

"We have only just arrived," said Emily's mother, from just behind Emily. "That is why –"

"I am certain that Lord Smithton does not need to know such things," Lord Chesterton interrupted, silencing Emily's mother immediately. "He is clearly grateful that Emily has not yet had her head turned by any other gentleman as yet."

Closing her eyes tightly, Emily forced herself to breathe normally, aware of how Lord Smithton chuckled at this. She did not have any feelings of attraction or even fondness for Lord Smithton but yet her father was stating outright that she was interested in Lord Smithton's attentions!

"I have chosen the quadrille, the waltz and the supper dance, Miss Taylor."

Emily's eyes shot open, and she practically jerked back the dance card from Lord Smithton's hands, preventing him from finishing writing his name in the final space. Her father stiffened beside her, her mother gasping in shock, but Emily did not allow either reaction to prevent her from keeping her dance card away from Lord Smithton.

"I am afraid I cannot permit such a thing, Lord Smithton," she told him plainly, her voice shaking as she struggled to find the confidence to speak with the strength she needed. "Three dances would, as you know, send many a tongue wagging and I cannot allow such a thing to happen. I am quite certain you will understand." She lifted her chin, her stomach twisting this way and that in fright as Lord Smithton narrowed his eyes and glared at her.

"My daughter is quite correct, Lord Smithton," Lady Chesterton added, settling a cold hand on Emily's shoulder. "Three dances are, as you know, something that the *ton* will notice and discuss without dissention."

Emily held her breath, seeing how her father and Lord Smithton exchanged a glance. Her eyes began to burn with unshed tears but she did not allow a single one to fall. She was trying to be strong, was she not? Therefore, she could not allow herself to show Lord Smithton even a single sign of weakness.

"I suppose that is to be understood," Lord Smithton said, eventually, forcing a breath of relief to escape from Emily's chest, weakening her. "Given that I have not made my intentions towards you clear, Miss Taylor."

The weakness within her grew all the more. "Intentions?" she repeated, seeing the slow smile spreading across Lord Smithton's face and feeling almost sick with the horror of what was to come.

Lord Smithton took a step closer to her and reached for her hand, which Emily was powerless to refuse. His eyes were fixed on hers, his tongue running across his lower lip for a moment before he spoke.

"Your father and I have been in discussions as regards your dowry and the like, Miss Taylor," he explained, his hand tightening on hers. "We should come to an agreement very soon, I am certain of it."

Emily closed her eyes tightly, feeling her mother's hand still resting on her shoulder and forcing herself to focus on it, to feel the support that she needed to manage this moment and all the emotions that came with it.

"We shall be wed before Season's end," Lord Smithton finished, grandly, as though Emily would be delighted with such news. "We shall be happy and content, shall we not, Miss Taylor?"

The lump in Emily's throat prevented her from saying anything. She wanted to tell Lord Smithton that he had not even asked her to wed him, had not considered her answer, but the words would not come to her lips. Of course, she would have no choice in the matter. Her father would make certain of that.

"You are speechless, of course," Lord Smithton chuckled, as her father grunted his approval. "I know that this will come as something of a surprise that I have denied myself towards marrying someone such as you, but I have no doubt that we shall get along rather famously." His chuckle became dark, his hand tightening on hers until it became almost painful. "You are an obedient sort, are you not?"

"She is," Emily heard her father say, as she opened her eyes to see Lord Smithton's gaze running over her form. She had little doubt as to what he was referring to, for her mother had already spoken to her about what a husband would require from his wife, and the very thought terrified her.

"Take her, now."

Lord Smithton let go of Emily's hand and gestured towards Lady Chesterton, as though she were his to order about.

"Take her to seek some refreshment. She looks somewhat pale." He laughed and then turned away to speak to Emily's father again, leaving Emily and her mother standing together.

Emily's breathing was becoming ragged, her heart trembling within her as she struggled to fight against the dark clouds that were filling her heart and mind. To be married to such an odious gentleman as Lord Smithton was utterly terrifying. She would have no joy in her life any longer, not even an ounce of happiness in her daily living. Was this her doing? Was it because she had not been strong enough to stand up to her own father and refuse to do as he asked? Her hands clenched hard, her eyes closing tightly as she fought to contain the sheer agony that was deep within her heart.

"My dear girl, I am so dreadfully sorry."

Lady Chesterton touched her arm but Emily jerked away, her eyes opening. "I cannot marry Lord Smithton, Mama."

"You have no choice," Lady Chesterton replied, sadly, her own eyes glistening. "I have tried to speak to your father but you know the sort of gentleman he is."

"Then I shall run away," Emily stated, fighting against the desperation that filled her. "I cannot remain."

Lady Chesterton said nothing for a moment or two, allowing Emily to realize the stupidity of what she had said. There was no-one else to whom she could turn to, no-one else to whom she might escape. The only choices that were open to her were either to do as her father asked or to find another who might marry her instead – and the latter gave her very little hope.

Unless Lord Havisham....

The thought was pushed out of her mind before she could begin to consider it. She had become acquainted with Lord Havisham over the few weeks she had been in London and he had appeared very attentive. He always sought her out to seek a dance or two, found her conversation engaging and had even called upon her on more than one occasion. But to ask him to consider marrying her was something that Emily simply could not contemplate. He would think her rude, foolish and entirely improper, particularly when she could not be certain that he had any true affection for her.

But if you do nothing, then Lord Smithton will have his way.

"Emily."

Her mother's voice pulled her back to where she stood, seeing the pity and the helplessness in her mother's eyes and finding herself filling with despair as she considered her future.

"I do not want to marry Lord Smithton," Emily said again, tremulously. "He is improper, rude and I find myself afraid of him." She saw her mother drop her head, clearly struggling to find any words to encourage Emily. "What am I to do, mama?"

"I – I do not know." Lady Chesterton looked up slowly, a single tear running down her cheek. "I would save you from this if I could, Emily but there is nothing I can do or say that will prevent your father from forcing this upon you."

Emily felt as though a vast, dark chasm had opened up underneath her feet, pulling her down into it until she could barely breathe. The shadows seemed to fill her lungs, reaching in to tug at her heart until it beat so quickly that she felt as though she might faint.

"I must go," Emily whispered, reaching out to grasp her mother's hand for a moment. "I need a few minutes alone." She did not wait for her mother to say anything, to give her consent or refusal, but hurried away without so much as a backward look. She walked blindly through the crowd of guests, not looking to the left or to the right but rather straight ahead, fixing her gaze on her goal. The open doors that led to the dark gardens.

The cool night air brushed at her hot cheeks but Emily barely noticed. Wrapping her arms about her waist, she hurried down the steps and then sped across the grass, not staying on the paths that wound through the gardens themselves. She did not know where she was going, only that she needed to find a small, dark, quiet space where she might allow herself to think and to cry without being seen.

She soon found it. A small arbor kept her enclosed as she sank down onto the small wooden bench. No sound other than that of strains of music and laughter from the ballroom reached her ears. Leaning forward, Emily felt herself begin to crumble from within, her heart aching and her mind filled with despair. There was no way out. There was nothing she could do. She would have to marry Lord Smithton and, in doing so, would bring herself more sadness and pain than she had ever felt before.

There was no-one to rescue her. There was no-one to save her. She was completely and utterly alone.

CHAPTER TWO

hree days later and Emily had stopped her weeping and was now staring at herself in the mirror, taking in the paleness of her cheeks and the dullness of her eyes.

Her father had only just now informed her that she was to be wed by the Season's end and was now to consider herself engaged. There had been no discussion. There had been not even a thought as to what she herself might feel as regarded Lord Smithton. It had simply been a matter of course. She was to do as her father had directed, as she had been taught to do.

Emily swallowed hard, closing her eyes tightly as another wave of tears crashed against her closed lids. Was this to be her end? Married to Lord Smithton, a gentleman whom she despised, and allowing herself to be treated in any way he chose? It would be a continuation of her life as it was now. No consideration, no thought was given to her. Expected to do as she was instructed without question – and no doubt the consequences would be severe for her if she did not do as Lord Smithton expected.

A shudder ran through her and Emily opened her eyes. For the first time, a small flickering flame of anger ignited and began to burn within her. Was she simply going to allow this to be her life? Was she merely going to step aside and allow Lord Smithton and her father to come to this arrangement without her acceptance? Was she truly as weak as all that?

Heat climbed up her spine and into her face. Weak was a word to describe her, yes. She *was* weak. She had tried, upon occasion, to do as she pleased instead of what her father had demanded of her and the punishment each time had broken her spirit all the more until she had not even a single thought about disobeying him. It had been what had led to this circumstance. If she had been stronger, if she had been more willing to accept the consequences of refusing to obey her father without question without allowing such a thing to break her spirit, then would she be as she was now?

"Then mayhap there is a time yet to change my circumstances."

The voice that came from her was weak and tremulous but with a lift of her chin, Emily told herself that she needed to try and find some courage if she was to find any hope of escaping Lord Smithton. And the only thought she had was that of Lord Havisham.

Viscount Havisham was, of course, lower in title and wealth than the Marquess of Smithton, but that did not matter to Emily. They had discovered a growing acquaintance between them, even though it was not often that her father had let her alone to dance and converse with another gentleman. It had been a blessing that the requests to call upon her had come at a time when her father had been resting from the events of the previous evening, for her and her mother had been able to arrange for him to call when Lord Chesterton had been gone from the house. However, nothing of consequence had ever been shared between them and he certainly had not, as yet, made his request to court her but mayhap it had simply been too soon for such a decision. Regardless, Emily could not pretend that they did not enjoy a comfortable acquaintance, with easy conversation and many warm glances shared between them. In truth, her heart fluttered whenever she laid eyes upon him, for his handsome features and his broad smile had a profound effect upon her.

It was her only chance to escape from Lord Smithton. She had to speak to Lord Havisham and lay her heart bare. She had to trust that he too had a fondness for her, in the same way that she had found her affections touched by him. Else what else was she to do?

Lifting her chin, Emily closed her eyes and took in a long breath to steady herself. After a moment of quiet reflection, she rose and made her way to the writing table in the corner of the bedchamber, sitting down carefully and picking up her quill.

"Miss Taylor."

Emily's breath caught as she looked up into Lord

Havisham's face. His dark blue eyes held a hint of concern, his smile somewhat tensed as he bowed in greeting.

"Lord Havisham," she breathed, finding even his very presence to be overwhelming. "You received my note, then."

"I did," he replied, with a quick smile, although a frown began to furrow his brow. "You said that it was of the utmost importance that we spoke this evening."

Emily nodded, looking about her and seeing that her father was making his way up the small staircase towards the card room, walking alongside Lord Smithton. Their engagement was to be announced later this evening and Emily knew she had to speak to Lord Havisham before that occurred.

"I know this is most untoward, but might we speak in private?" she asked, reaching out and surreptitiously putting her hand on his arm, battling against the fear of impropriety. She had done this much, she told herself. Therefore, all she had to do was continue on as she had begun and her courage might be rewarded.

Lord Havisham hesitated. "That may be a little...."

Emily blushed furiously, knowing that to speak alone with a gentleman was not at all correct, for it could bring damaging consequences to them both – but for her, at this moment, she did not find it to be a particularly concerning issue, given that she was to be married to Lord Smithton if he did not do anything.

"It is of the greatest importance, as I have said," she replied, quickly, praying that he would consent. "Please, Lord Havisham, it will not take up more than a few minutes of your time." Seeing him hesitate even more, she bit her lip. "Surely you must know me well enough to know that I would not force you into anything, Lord Havisham," she pleaded, noting how his eyes darted away from hers, a slight flush now in his cheeks. "There is enough of a friendship between us, is there not?"

Lord Havisham nodded and then sighed "I am sorry, Miss Taylor," he replied, quietly, looking at her. "You are quite right. Come. The gardens will be quiet."

Walking away from her mother – who did not do anything to hinder Emily's departure, Emily felt such an overwhelming sense of relief that it was all she could do to keep her composure. Surely Lord Havisham, with his goodness and kind nature, would see the struggle that faced her and seek to do what he could to bring her aid? Surely he had something of an affection in his heart for her? But would it be enough?

"Now," Lord Havisham began, as they stepped outside. "What is it that troubles you so, Miss Taylor?"

Now that it came to it, Emily found her mouth going dry and her heart pounding so furiously that she could barely speak. She looked up at Lord Havisham, seeing his features only slightly in the darkness of the evening and found herself desperately trying to say even a single word.

"It is....." Closing her eyes, she halted and dragged in air, knowing that she was making a complete cake of herself.

"I am to be wed to Lord Smithton," she managed to say, her words tumbling over each other in an attempt to be spoken. "I have no wish to marry him but my father insists upon it." Opening her eyes, she glanced warily up at Lord Havisham and saw his expression freeze.

Find out what happens next between Emily and Lord Havisham in the book, available in the Kindle Store A New Beginning

JOIN MY MAILING LIST

Sign up for my newsletter to stay up to date on new releases, contests, giveaways, freebies, and deals!

Free book with signup!

Monthly Facebook Giveaways! Books and Amazon gift cards!
Join me on Facebook: https://www.
facebook.com/rosepearsonauthor

Website: www.RosePearsonAuthor.com

Follow me on Goodreads: Author Page

You can also follow me on Bookbub!
Click on the picture below – see the Follow button?